I0524016

Additional praise for

Gathered Here Together
STORIES

"Garrett Socol looks benignly on our mucky world and conveys the dark humour of everyday madness."

—*Nth Position*

"There's no question that Garrett Socol can tell a good story, weaving subtle plots and intriguing characters together with skill and sophistication. But for us, what takes his work to the next level is his often wry observation of contemporary society, his ear for surprising language and phrases that just leap out of the page at the reader, and his obvious love of exploring frequently quite complex ideas. Whenever we start reading a Garrett Socol story, we know it's going to challenge us and make us think - and work like that is all too rare."

— *> kill author*

Gathered Here Together

Stories

Garrett Socol

Copyright © 2011 Garrett Socol. All rights reserved.

No portion of this work may be reproduced by any means without the express written permission of the publisher, except short passages excerpted for academic or review purposes.

This is a work of fiction. All characters are products of the author's imagination, and any resemblance to any actual people is coincidence.

Cover art "Choice" copyright © 2011 Tommy Ingberg. All rights reserved.

Book design by Pequod Book Design, www.pequodbookdesign.com

ISBN: 978-0-9841025-7-0

Edited by Stephanie Renae Johnson. Special thanks to Tyler Gillespie, and Claire Thurmon-Bryan.

Additional thanks to the following publications, where many of these stories first appeared.

The Barcelona Review, Spork Press, JMWW, Pequin, The 2nd Hand, Paradigm, Matchbook, The Medulla Review, Ducts, Underground Voices, > kill author, 3:AM Magazine, Nth Position, Hobart, Perigee, The Northville Review, Emprise Review, and *Word Riot*

In memory of Bud Douglass

Contents

Gathered Here Together: Stories

Sally's Suicide Checklist

RETURNING HOME AFTER HAVING HER STOMACH PUMPED was not one of Sally Biddle's favorite activities. The food in her refrigerator would be growing mold, the toilet seat in her bathroom would be freezing cold, and more often than not, dried blood would have to be hand-washed from the hickory hardwood floor in the living room. But here she was again, in the passenger seat of Adam Delgado's white Infiniti, with its tinted windows and new car scent, pulling up to her empty duplex.

"If a dozen people are on the other side of the door waiting to scream 'Surprise,' I won't speak to you for six months," she warned.

"I'd never let a dozen people see you looking like such hell," he assured her, clutching her arm to keep her from falling and breaking some bone on the winding brick path. "You look like you just spent two weeks at Buchenwald."

The thick bushes and monster fica trees surrounding the place seemed more unkempt and overgrown than Sally remembered. "I forgot that I live in a jungle," she joked. "Do ferocious animals roam about?"

"A few wild bears and some wild boars, that's all."

"I've met the boars. They are so boring," she said. Then, "Oh my God!" She grabbed the back of Adam's neck like a metal harness on a bus, dangling from above. This startled reaction had nothing to do with the frenetic foliage or her housekeeping needs. The sight of eight newspapers haphazardly piled on her welcome mat threw Sally into a panic. She stared at the dated editions of *The New York Times* and *Orange County Register* with outright horror. "I was away four days, and it looks like I've been gone four months."

"That's because you get two newspapers delivered daily when most people only get none," Adam responded with a shrug.

"But do you know what this means?" she asked.

"Sure. You have some catching up do to on world news, not to mention the latest gossip." He tried to sound undaunted by his closest friend's brush with the beyond.

"Adam," Sally scolded, "I might as well have tacked up a sign saying *Not Home,* with a giant arrow pointing to my door. Some thief could've broken in and hit the road with my pills." She didn't seem the least bit concerned about her computer, furniture, flat screen TV, diamond necklace, first-edition copy of *Love in the Time of Cholera*, giant exercise ball, sterling silver asparagus tongs, or even the thousand dollars in cash stored in a box of animal crackers in the kitchen cabinet.

"I guess you'll have to hide those babies very carefully the next time you get carted away," Adam said with more than a little sarcasm.

This particular hospital visit had occurred immediately after Jill DeHaven Arvisse found Sally unconscious on the living room floor with blood trickling from her mouth in a raindrop-shaped puddle of maroon. Sally had swallowed one or two or four too many oval white pills along with more than several tiny yellow ones. After the pumping of her stomach, Dr. Eve McNeal suggested a few days in the Middleditch Mental Health Facility for observation. "I could think of more interesting people to observe," Sally told her therapist. "Why don't you call the French Rugby Team?"

During the previous year, Sally had made a strong and semi-successful effort to reduce the number of tablets she took on a regular basis. On her last visit, Dr. McNeal congratulated her on a fifty percent reduction, but reminded her that there was another fifty to go. "That second fifty can be tough," she'd warned.

"Bet it's a real bitch," Sally had responded.

Adam watched Sally toss her bag on the floor, step out of her shoes, and plop down on her sofa. A long sigh emerged from her weak, weary body. "Thanks for getting me home in one piece," she said.

"Sure you'll be all right by yourself?" he asked.

"Of course. Slitting my wrists is the farthest thing from my mind, unless Jill DeHaven Arvisse calls."

"Hey, if it wasn't for Jill DeHaven Arvisse, you'd probably be dead."

"Very true," Sally admitted. "If she didn't insist on picking me up for our Friday mani-pedis, I'd still be lying on that living room floor. Dead in the *living* room. Does the name of the room change when death is involved?"

"Don't think so," Adam said. "The dead room doesn't feel right."

"The Dead Room," Sally repeated. "Sounds like a Stephen King novel."

"It does," he replied pensively. "I'm just curious. Did Jill DeHaven Arvisse get her nails done after you were carried away by the paramedics?"

"I wouldn't say I was *carried away* by them. One was kind of cute, the other wasn't my type. But to answer your question, I'm so sure Jill DeHaven Arvisse went to her appointment that I would bet my prescription medication on it."

"Then I have no doubt."

"Good, because if you think she'd allow a little thing like my overdose ruin her mani-pedi, you don't have a very good sense of the bitch." They'd known Jill since all three were sophomores at San Francisco State, trudging through Fundamentals of Literary Analysis, when she was just plain Jill DeHaven. Since marrying Julian Arvisse (a postdoctoral research fellow), adding his name to hers and becoming a major snob, Sally and Adam never referred to Jill without using all three names. "I'm in no mood for Jill DeHaven Arvisse's advice right now."

"I don't blame you. She's going to invite you to her End of Summer party, by the way," Adam warned Sally as he massaged her socked foot.

"Uh, should someone remind her that it's only June?"

"You know how much she hates summer. She decided to acknowledge the season for two weeks, then pretend fall came early this year."

"And they sent *me* to a nut ward," Sally mumbled.

Adam kissed her on the cheek and embraced her the way a deeply caring gay friend embraces a beloved straight one who just survived a close encounter with mortality. "Love you more than my laptop," he said. This was his catch phrase for Sally, and Sally only.

"I don't know why. It's sleek, slim, dependable, and couldn't ingest a pill if it *tried*," she sighed. "C'mon, I'll walk you out."

"Stay right here. You need to take it easy, give your body a rest. Maybe start writing another magazine article, or even a book." He stepped over eight newspapers, a brown leather bag and a couple of decorative throw pillows to get to the front door. "I'll call you later, doll."

"Please do," she called back.

When he was gone, she closed her eyes and remained still for a solid minute and a half. When she opened them, she focused on the heap of newspapers. There was something about the mound of black and white print, its sheer volume, its valuable information, that struck her in a curious way. Slowly, she stood up and mounted the narrow carpeted staircase to her second-story bedroom. A framed photograph of her mother, Renata, taken shortly before she died, greeted Sally at the top of the stairs. Sally had always wished she looked less like her pale, thin English father and more like her dark-eyed, voluptuous Spanish mom. She grabbed a pen and a pad of paper, and parked herself in her large wicker chair facing the window, a sliver of ocean in the distance. The pile of old newspapers meant something, were somehow connected to her recent ordeal. With a magazine article in mind, she began writing.

It was obvious the delivery of these papers should have been stopped, but this was merely the tip of a gigantic iceberg, an iceberg she'd never noticed until now. If she had really intended to kill herself, there were a host of tasks that should've been addressed – canceling magazine subscriptions, watering plants in excess, and alerting credit card companies to the fact that any forthcoming charges would be fraudulent. A truly determined Sally realized how invaluable a suicide checklist would be to future suicidal folk. But it would be more than a mere list; it would be a detailed record, embellished with abundant and humorous commentary, of responsibilities to be dealt with before any slitting of wrists, ingesting of pills, or blasting of bullets would take place.

The landline rattled like a fire alarm. (She was the only person she knew who still *had* one.) Sally screeched as the pad of paper flew out of her hands.

"Hello," she answered, voice quivering, searching for the ringer's volume control as she spoke.

"Sally," Trevor responded. Trevor Bloom, the heartbreaker. "I heard you were back from the hospital. How are you doing?" She hadn't heard from him in months and was finally moving forward, but the mere sound of his deep voice sent her reeling back, tumbling toward her sickbed of obsession.

"I'm feeling good," she chirped. "Just got back, so you can imagine there are a million things to do."

"Only *one* million?"

She forced a chuckle. "Right. More like two or three. I don't even know where to start." It was clear the only way to protect herself was to avoid him. "I appreciate the call, Trevor, but I need to run." With that, she gently pulled the plug out of the wall.

Her heart was pounding so furiously it felt like it would break open her chest. (She hadn't felt such a powerful jolt since the time she visited her family home in Phoenix and saw that her old bedroom had been turned into an office.) She still loved him deeply and desired him desperately, but he wasn't ready for that all-consuming thing Sally wanted with him, something she hadn't wanted with anyone else, ever, in her entire young life. Trevor said he loved her but he always kept one foot out the door, a single Nike waiting for him on the welcome mat. She wanted to take that shoe and shove it into a burning fireplace.

"Back to the issue at hand," she barked an order to herself. She fired up her computer and continued, carried by a sense of importance. Words gushed out of her like water from a broken dam:

> *It's imperative to temporarily ignore agonizing feelings of hopelessness, futility and despair in order to put your affairs in order. You need to focus on the following matters in order to enjoy a smooth ride into eternity: Find new homes for pets. Cancel all newspaper and magazine subscriptions. Pay off credit card debts. Alert post office that mail should be "returned to sender." Delete embarrassing items from computer. Clean out closets and dressers in every single room; do you really want someone examining your toiletries, underwear, and old tax returns?*

One idea morphed into the next. Sally lost herself in this for hours, marveling at the fact that writing about death could generate such a surge of life.

Some people travel to a foreign country when they feel the time has come to stop participating with the living. Once they've reached their exotic destination, they destroy identifying documents (passport, driver license). Some choose the comfort of their hotel suite in which to swallow a few dozen pills. (Luxury hotels know how to deal with the aftermath of this sort of thing.) Others hop a train to a remote village. This way, the authorities (or tribal chief) won't know who you are, where you were born or what kind of music you like. They'll declare you a Jane or John Doe (or a Jumaane or Jumaan Dabulamanzi) and bury your body in an unmarked grave. To the folks back home, you're merely off on some lengthy, wild adventure.

Sally clearly stated that suicide should only be considered as a last resort, and she made a point to discourage these ideas in children, animals, and anyone who has a hefty inheritance coming his or her way.

The ancient Greeks believed that the manner of one's death is as important as the substance of one's life. Therefore, it's wise to select just the right location in which to end your physical existence. Classy choice: "The body was discovered in the Executive Suite of New York's Peninsula Hotel." Sordid choice: "The body was found in a room at the Motel 6 just outside Mobile, Alabama."

After completing the first few chapters of her book, which she decided to call *Sally's Suicide Checklist,* she sent them to her agent Saffron Preminger. "I adore this project," Saffron wrote in an e-mail. "It's fun, funny, and could be a useful tool to a lot of people who buy books. It's always the intelligent ones who kill themselves – Spalding Gray,

Sylvia Plath, David Foster Wallace. Tragic." Two weeks later, Saffron closed a deal with a small but respected publishing company, and Adam suggested a huge book party to celebrate.

"I don't think I have enough friends for a party," Sally pouted. "It's pathetic."

"You've got plenty of friends," he told her. "But I have an even better idea. Let's go to Jill DeHaven Arvisse's End of Summer shindig next week and have our own party within a party. Save us the cost of refreshments and decor."

Sally lit up. "Sometimes your brilliance boggles my mind."

The End of Summer party was in full swing under the recessed lighting of Jill DeHaven Arvisse's spacious living room. The house was in one of the country's most exclusive zip codes, a posh neighborhood bespotted with BMWs, Ferraris, and mansions in the five million dollar range. The Arvisse residence was professionally decorated with textured white walls, plush white carpet and ubiquitous white roses, not a yellow one in the bunch. The house seemed like a floating cumulus cloud.

The catering company was the most *au courant*. The kitchen was a hubbub of activity as four caterers prepared two lasagnas – one meat, one vegetarian – as well as a dozen smaller dishes including Swedish meatballs, Cajun shrimp, bison carpaccio, and braised Savoy cabbage. Guests included affluent members of the community: two cosmetic surgeons, several CEOs, one CFO, a Superior Court judge, a handful of attorneys, a bank president, conductor of the local symphony, and the Dean of Academic Affairs at UCLA. There were noticeably few people of color.

Inside, Armani-clad straight people sipped Dom Perignon while chatting about children and hedge funds. Outside, the dark pine deck overlooking the ocean was peopled with guests nibbling on nuts and Parmesan crisps while holding emerald green drinks in martini glasses.

In the cozy den down the hall, a more private affair was in progress. Sally held court in a silk camisole dress and plum suede pumps. Tall and lean in a button-down black shirt and dress pants, Adam looked ready to strut down a designer's catwalk. His wisecracking colleagues at the pet health clinic, Dax and Piper, were equally decked out and feeling positively giddy. All drank champagne and Chardonnay while sharing fantasies of murdering Jill DeHaven Arvisse and making it look like a suicide.

"I like the idea of starving her to death since she's halfway there anyway," Sally mused.

Adam lit up. "We kidnap the skinny bitch, tie her up, and let nature take its course." Just as he was about to share another inspired thought, the hostess herself materialized in the door frame with a goat cheese stuffed radish in her hand and an expression of horror.

"I cannot believe my eyes," Jill DeHaven Arvisse snapped in a state of quasi-hysteria, as everyone stared at her pink outfit, a formal prom gown gone wrong. "Do you realize who's attending my party? The most influential members of our community are mingling in the other room, including Jennifer Aniston's personal stylist, and you're hiding out in the den. It's unthinkably rude and frankly rather stupid."

"We were planning to make a move very soon," Sally reassured her.

"I'd appreciate it if you made that move right *now*," she said. "You won't get many chances to talk to these people, you should take advantage of the opportunity, all of you. And try the shaved asparagus with smoked trout and pistachios. *If* there are any left."

The galling, garrulous diva tossed her head back and rushed away. Nobody told her she had lipstick on her teeth.

An obscenity formed on Sally's lips, but she decided to keep it to herself. Instead she asked, "How did she turn into *that*? She used to be fairly pleasant."

"It happened over a short period of time," Adam said, "like a banana going brown."

"What does Jennifer Aniston's stylist do?" Piper wondered. "She's had the same style for fifteen years."

Sally roused herself to her feet. "Let's mingle. We might never have a chance to talk to these people again," she added sarcastically.

The gang marched into the living room where they were bombarded by a virtual wall of garlic. Two tall women in white aprons were serving lasagna on a white-draped table in the nearby dining room. Sally and friends weaved through the crowd until they reached the deck, out of the garlic and into the ocean salt. The mammoth Pacific seemed like a painted backdrop, a spectacular piece of scenery that Jill DeHaven Arvisse might have rented for the night.

Just hours earlier, the water was azure; now it shimmered black. Sally watched a surfer emerge from the water, even though the ocean was placid, offering little chance of encountering that awesome wave. She was the surfer in her own crazy life, waiting for something life-changing to show its face. Sally merely mingled with friends, lovers, pills, therapy, a promising but stalled career. She was riding the sometimes calm, sometimes choppy water, waiting, waiting. Dr. McNeal had prescribed antidepressants. They worked for a while, then stopped. She prescribed different ones. They worked for a while, then stopped. Sally concluded that most people were born right, but she was born wrong, defective. Her wave never came.

Sally's reverie was interrupted by a gasp from Adam. "Don't move," he whispered into Sally's ear. "Trevor's in the house."

Shaking her head in disbelief, Sally whispered, "How the hell could she invite Trevor? How could that insensitive bitch? She knew I was coming!"

"Because she's an insensitive bitch," Adam whispered back.

"I'm leaving."

"No. Be strong. You look gorgeous."

"I don't know if I can take it."

"I'll be at your side."

"Do I really look gorgeous?"

"Yes you do," Adam told her, giving her a squeeze. "Tiny warning: he's not alone."

Sally took her time turning around, as if moving at a snail's pace would somehow alter the situation. Then she saw him – charismatic as ever, his eye candy a pencil-thin princess with flowing blonde hair. Sally studied him for a few seconds before he noticed her, and when he did, his face lit up. She hoped he wouldn't feel the need to creep through the crowd and converse. But creep he did, bony babe in tow, eager for conversation.

"Hey Sally, you look fantastic," Trevor gushed, as if he expected her to appear haggard or pock-marked, possibly spasmodic. "You even have a decent tan."

"Thanks," she managed to say despite her thumping heart.

"I want you to meet Kym." .

"Hello, Kym," Sally said, feeling like an ugly, overweight stepsister.

"Hey," she replied, slightly woozy. "It's Kym with a y, by the way."

"Then we have something in common besides Trevor. I'm *Sally* with a y."

"Oh cool," Kym said. Sally's offbeat sense of humor flew miles over her head.

Sally wasn't sure what she loathed more: Kym's perky breasts or mile-long legs. She looked into Trevor's hollow eyes and acknowledged the meager remains of their mercurial relationship: a smile, a few words, a sense of caring, but only up to a point. Embers glowed, but Trevor obviously found his fierce, red- hot fire in a partially hydrogenated blonde with partially exposed breasts and – if first impressions were accurate – partial intelligence.

"If Lil' Kym lost any more weight, she wouldn't *be* there," Adam whispered into Sally's ear, pulling her a foot away. She erupted into nervous laughter.

"You have to admit he looks great since he dumped me," Sally whispered back. She was glad she'd taken a cue from Anne Sexton who never ventured anywhere without "kill-me pills" in her purse. Suddenly, Jill DeHaven Arvisse called for everyone's attention.

All eyes turned to the living room where Jill stood next to her husband – the tall, taciturn Julian Arvisse – against the white marble fireplace. With their pale skin and pouting mouths, they looked eerily like siblings. When Jill was satisfied with the level of stillness, she cleared her throat, lifted her hand pretentiously, and delivered the announcement: "We're pregnant."

Cheers and whoops rocked the place, along with some serious jumping up and down. "I *thought* she looked a little chunky," Adam whispered.

"That poor fetus," Sally added. "Can you imagine having Jill DeHaven Arvisse guiding you through life?"

"The moment that baby's born, we should warn it."

"Let's take it to lunch on its one-month birthday."

"I'd bet serious cash you could use a drink about now, darling," Adam said, eyeing Sally's hand, white-knuckled on the balcony rail.

"Good guess. Martini, please. With a cyanide chaser."

"Coming right up."

Sally glanced at the ocean and saw a very different, very tranquil world. Heart still racing, she hobbled to the door of the deck, unlatched the lock, removed her shoes, and stepped down to the sand, which was colder than she expected. Walking toward the water, she shut her eyes and stretched her arms horizontally, offering herself to the night.

Something was certainly wrong; the pieces of Sally's life had never come together the way they had for Jill DeHaven Arvisse and everyone else she knew. These people relished their systematic, sun-dappled lives; they couldn't wait to wake up in the morning. Sally dreaded the infinite sadness the day would bring. She'd searched for love and almost found it. She'd wanted to be a great writer, but her two published books *(The Occasional Caucasian* and *Condiments for Cannibals)* were only modest successes. Her newest, *Sally's Suicide Checklist,* was a nominal source of excitement, but there were no guarantees. She'd been climbing the mountain for such a long time, desperately wanting to find herself at the apex but consistently forced to start over at the bottom, empty-handed...except for her pills. Her pills made her feel whole, happy, worthwhile. Her painkillers did what they were supposed to do: *they killed her pain.* They brought relief and joy. But everyone told her to stop taking them because they were killing more than her pain. So she obeyed. She cut down by half. And her joy was cut in half. Her will to live was cut in half, and she honestly didn't know if this was a good trade.

Close to the water, she breathed deeply and wondered how cold the water would be. It turned out to be *ice* cold, sending shivers along her spine. But it was also magically alive – moving, swishing, enjoying its unique, never-ending dance without interference. The water swallowed her feet and ankles; she waited out the chill, knowing her body would adjust to the temperature.

There were no big waves at this hour, just rolls of water rushing to the shore and then dissolving, silent pleats of horizontal whiteness that looked like neon strips across the sea, connecting north with south. Sally stood perfectly still, allowing the sights, sounds and smells of the Pacific to fill her to the gills, letting the foamy spray of the ocean brush her feet and ankles, cool and tingle them.

A quick glance at the house turned into a lingering stare; the party seemed surprisingly far away, its muted light a speck in the distance. Still, she knew an entire universe existed there: civilized albeit boring adults with jobs and jewelry and timeshares were engaging in what they considered interesting conversation, taking themselves very seriously. She heard distant laughter. This was a place that welcomed Sally as a guest but rejected her as a resident. She remained at the children's table, watching the grown-ups from afar, the motherless teenager on Mother's Day.

A strong surge of cold water unexpectedly hit Sally's knees, as if deliberately playing with her. This made her laugh out loud; her sadness evaporated like a mist. With a renewed sense of purpose, she marched back to the house, knowing she wouldn't stay long. Adam was waiting for her on the deck with a martini.

"Your martini," he said. "It's apple."

"You know I love you, right?" She kissed him on the cheek before he accompanied her back into the bustle of the living room.

"I think I know that."

By this time, almost everyone had imbibed two or three too many cocktails. The cacophony of the party – laughing, droning, yelling, yammering, even the music – was blaring and obnoxious, and the room still reeked of garlic. Sally felt entirely out of place. Just before midnight, she slipped out the front door, as some wobbly guests had been routinely doing for fresh air or a quick smoke.

A blissful silence greeted her like a shot of morphine. She strolled down the wide street with its impressive mansions and immaculate lawns and the smell of jasmine. The clacking of her heels on the pavement, a metallic tick tock that always reminded her of her mother, was the only sound for miles. Her stride was lithe and confident, and each step brought her closer to the place she needed to be, to the discovery she had to make. Though slightly wasted from the gin, the noise, one valium, and Trevor, she felt unfettered and in control, knowing it was time to fuse with something, someone, someplace, in the universe.

Two weeks later, when no one had heard a word from Sally, Adam concluded that she either quietly killed herself or took a trip to a faraway place. He didn't panic because, as much as he'd miss her, he knew that Sally believed suicide, in certain cases, was the right decision. He began to go through the necessary motions, using the copy of *Sally's Suicide Checklist* that she had given him, though he knew what he would find.

Cancel all newspaper and magazine subscriptions. It had already been done.

Clean out closets and dressers in every room. (Do you really want someone examining your toiletries, underwear, and old tax returns?) It, too, had been done.

Alert post office that mail should be "returned to sender." This had also been accomplished.

Sally had followed her own guidelines to a tee.

Adam clung to the notion that Sally voluntarily disappeared and was on the journey of her lifetime. That was how he managed to get through this. Over and over, he told himself Sally was alive, and at a certain point, he began to believe it.

One year later, *Sally's Suicide Checklist* hit the *New York Times* bestseller list at number three. No one paid much attention to a small chapter toward the end of the book. It read, in part:

> *If you could move to a different city and live anonymously for a year, what would life be like? For instance, you pick up and go to the South of France. Or the North Pole. Or the south of North Dakota. Or the north of Southampton; it doesn't matter. The important factor is that nobody knows you. You're an intriguing new face, with a refreshingly clean slate. Would you enjoy the experience?*

Sally Biddle found a small, elegantly furnished apartment not far from Plaza Catalunya in bustling Barcelona, the birthplace of her mother. Vibrant, restless Las Ramblas, the haunting Sagrada Familia, the lively beaches of Bogatell and Mar Bella, the biking on La Diagonal, the food, the fun, the spirit – Sally had the vague sense this could be home. She knew that when the time was right, she would contact Adam, and make him smile with joy.

Gathered Here Together

Traffic was light at 8:40 in the evening, so Trish London's drive in the purple rental car would have been pleasant if not for the record-breaking temperature. The entire state of Ohio was under the iron thumb of an oppressive heat wave which, according to local meteorologists, would rule for at least five or six days. The AC in the sedan didn't work, so Trish barreled down the freeway with all four windows open in an attempt to avoid suffocation.

The wind whipped in Trish's hair as she passed the familiar towns of Millbury, Glumm, and Coal Grove, feeling like an animal being led to slaughter. She was heading toward parents and a home from which she had escaped four years earlier. Her heart raced and body tensed when the *Welcome to Two Rivers* sign loomed. The purpose of this homecoming was not to come home; home just happened to be in the neighborhood, and it was cheaper than a room at the Ramada. But Trish tried to focus on the bright side: she'd be flying back to New York in just 36 hours. She already missed her professors at NYU as well as her pals at the ad agency.

The house of her childhood seemed smaller, the front lawn shrunken. She feared her head might hit the ceiling. Trish wondered if her parents had morphed into marionettes during her time away. Parking behind her father's dusty old Chevy truck, she lost nineteen years and became six again, sitting in the high front seat that made her feel like she was riding an elephant.

Pushing against a dread more oppressive than the heat, Trish climbed out of the car. Her legs moved slowly, against their will. Leaning against the rental, she gazed at the glowing quarter moon, the only speck of brightness in a gloomy, cavernous landscape. She closed her eyes, wishing she could do anything but walk the plank that awaited her.

She forced herself to move, one foot following the other on the gravel, then the grass. Dead woman walking.

The mother of the deceased, in a black dress and humongous black hat half the size of the casket, carried on with the energy of a cruise director. She wept, whispered, wiped lint, paced, embraced, clasped her hands, passed out breath mints, pointed to the restroom, hugged, huddled, hydrated, and repeatedly checked her reflection in the church's window. Her actions didn't seem like those of a sane human being, or perhaps it was the breakneck speed with which she *performed* these actions that suggested a degree of insanity (or amphetamines).

Honey Frick wasn't an unattractive woman, but middle-age bloat made her chubby and awkward, uncomfortable with the mass of added weight. Her skin was alarmingly pale, as if she feared sunlight, and her choice of bright red lipstick was a serious mistake. From afar, she looked like an albino with a smear of blood for a mouth. The hat concealed lifeless hair, gray with hazelnut highlights. Lorelei's murder hadn't come as a complete shock to Honey, who equated life in New York City with danger, decadence, and death.

"How many times did I warn her?" she whispered to the mourners offering their condolences. "I told her that damn place was teeming with lunatics and troublemakers and it was only a matter of time before they struck a small town girl."

The sun was hidden behind thick, dark, slow-moving clouds, but its heat made the somber crowd sweat through the fancy Sunday clothes worn on this melancholy Saturday morning. The weather was all anybody could talk about: heat rash, heat cramps, rolling blackouts, wilted gardens, humidity, hyperthermia, dehydrated seniors, and the stench coming from Dumpsters filling up with spoiled food from refrigerators whose power had failed.

"They say it's going to cool down by the middle of next week," Honey's cheerful friend Danielle told her, hands clasped victoriously across her chest.

"They've been saying that for a month. Those idiots would predict sunshine in Seattle." Thunder sounded from somewhere in the distance. "Oh that's all we need, a frigging rainstorm."

"Might cool things off," Danielle suggested.

"Two or three degrees? I'd rather stay dry."

Scanning the crowd, Honey audibly gasped when she spotted Trish London. It was a loud, jarring rip separating one moment from the next, before and after, pre and post. Remembering her manners, Honey closed her mouth. All things considered, this difficult morning had been going smoothly, but now a thorn had been thrust into Honey's behind, and the sting was excruciating. Trish awkwardly put her arms around the mother of her late best friend. "I'm so very sorry," she murmured.

"You decided to fly in," Honey declared with artificial cheer.

"Of course I did," Trish replied, not surprised to smell booze on Honey's breath. "We were so close."

"Friends and family will be stopping at the house after the

service," Honey said out of obligation. "But I know you're a vegetarian and we're serving an *abundance* of beef." The hostility was tangible.

"Oh," Trish responded, "Well, I don't exac-".

"Excuse me, dear." Honey abruptly stepped away to greet the town's most popular piano teacher. "Toluca!"

Falling into Honey's waiting arms, Toluca Weakland became a puddle of tears. "This isn't the way it's supposed to be," the petite woman sobbed. "A mother should go *before* her child. This should be *your* funeral, not Lorelei's."

"I'll second that," Trish muttered. She began to mill about as unobtrusively as possible. Even though these were the neighbors she'd known for the first eighteen years of her life, she strolled among them virtually unrecognized. A change of hair color and loss of forty pounds brought about a startling new look for Trish. Lorelei's lanky, blue-eyed brother Jesse kept glancing at her, scrutinizing her with a glimmer of recognition.

"You look so familiar," he finally admitted.

"Hi Jesse. It's Trish."

"Trish London?" he exclaimed. "Wow, you look fantastic! Not that you didn't look great before, but you got skinny and your hair is different. Wow. OK, no more wows, I promise. You flew in from New York?"

"Landed last night. How've you been?"

"Hanging in there," he beamed. "How 'bout you?"

"I've been better."

"Yeah, of course. Hey, do the police still think it was a random act of violence?"

"Totally random. But at least they *caught* the fucker. Wasn't the first time he did this." Trish took another glance at the growing crowd. "Don't tell me Lorelei knew all these people."

"Hell no."

"Then why are they here?"

"There's not a lot to do in this town, remember?"

"So because there's no zoo or water park, everybody dresses up and goes to a funeral?" she asked.

"The murder was a big deal," Jesse explained. "This is the event of the season."

"Oh. Well," Trish snapped, "I'm sure your sister's smiling from above, happy to provide a day of fun for the neighborhood folk."

"Listen," Jesse grinned, "My parents are having people over after the service. Why don't you come by and we can hang out?"

"Because I need to hang out with my own parents, as much as I wouldn't like to. They were asleep when I got in last night, and my plane leaves early tomorrow morning."

"Then come over for an hour. I was just a kid when you left." He wiped the sweat from his forehead. "We hardly knew each other."

"And now you're all grown-up."

"Sure am," he said with that teenage bravado. "Every inch of me."

"Is that so?" she asked after a pause, slightly taken aback by his blatancy. She remembered the shy, gawky teenager with acne, much different from the clear-skinned, hot young man making himself as available as coffee at Starbucks. Fooling around with him was an enticing idea, until she realized how profoundly and perversely inappropriate it would be. Still, that didn't stop her from entertaining the notion. "What are you, eighteen? Nineteen?"

"I'll be twenty in June."

"June is ten months away, Jesse." The intellectual development didn't exactly match the physical, but that didn't bother her. If anything, it made him more attractive, more boyish and innocent than the arrogant Nietzsche-spewing seniors at NYU. "What do you say we head into the chapel?"

"Cool. Sit with me?"

"Are you freaking nuts? You need to sit up front with your family," Trish said. "I'll be in the back."

"All right."

The mourners filed in, a laborious process, as if lugging their bodies around in the heat was a Herculean struggle. The chapel was cramped and close, and made breathing difficult. Scents of perfume and sweat mingled in the air. Soft moaning and murmuring deflated into silence as a silver-haired minister, just this side of ancient, stepped to the lectern. He spoke lovingly and asthmatically of Lorelei despite admitting that he didn't remember the least bit about her. After a few puffs from his inhaler, he introduced Lorelei's father.

Aaron Frick, a tall, thin man who usually hid behind his brown frames and thick lenses, boasted about his daughter's early inquisitiveness. "At five or six, she asked, 'Why do we drive on parkways and park on driveways? How do I know you're not a figment of my imagination? Why are they called apartments when they're all stuck together?' Well, maybe she was seven." He adjusted his glasses and wiped the abundant sweat from his mouth and neck. He called for his son.

Jesse stepped up and expressed regret that his sister didn't take the time to get to know him before moving away. He went on to say that she was still a "cool sibling" and he missed her. Then he introduced his mother as "the woman who named her daughter Lorelei, which Lorelei never forgave her for." A few people chuckled. Honey shot poison darts straight from her eyes to those of her only living child. Then she hauled herself to the podium; her dramatic hat seemed to arrive several seconds before *she* did.

"I'm too saddened with grief to speak for long," she announced in a voice choked with tears (fake or real, Trish couldn't discern), "but I have a message to impart." She took a dramatic pause, obviously relishing her temporary stardom. "When my baby girl turned eighteen, she entered a rebellious stage and wanted to move to New York City. I pleaded with her to stay in Two Rivers, but when you're eighteen, the advice of a mother doesn't count for much. She wanted the glamorous life: fancy restaurants, opening nights, martinis with young men. She made a choice and followed her best friend to the Big Apple. Some of you might remember that friend, Trash London, Irene and Norm's girl. She always had a knack for shaking things up. Anyway, she lost a few pounds and flew from Fun City to partake in today's service. I'm sure she'd like to say a few words about my sweet deceased daughter whose death would not have occurred if it weren't for *her*. Trish London, everybody."

Mortified, Trish struggled up from her seat and proceeded to take the most grueling, wobbly walk of her life. Her limbs were lead. The only sound in the chapel was that of her heels clacking on the tiles, the metallic noise bouncing off the floor and hitting the ceiling where it split and slammed into the walls on its way down.

Standing behind the lectern with tremulous fear, heart beating in her head, her eyes met Honey's. *You demented bitch,* Trish thought. Jesse was gazing with lust. *He's picturing me naked right now.* Several parents covered the ears of their children to ward off the foul language that would surely spew from the mouth of the evil city-woman. Trish silently wished them all a safe trip to hell.

"I uh…I have to tell you that Honey is right," Trish announced to the somber crowd. "Lorelei moved to New York four years ago because of me. She was excited about her future, felt like it had so much potential. And it did. *She* did. We shared an apartment in Greenwich Village and had a ball, especially during Fleet Week." She hoped to hear a few laughs, but her remark was met with silence. A car alarm blasted outside, drowning out what she would have said. A handful of people stood up and rushed out from their pews.

Twenty seconds later, Trish continued speaking.

"To continue: Loree rarely ventured to the Upper East Side of Manhattan, but that's where the incident took place. A bad occurrence in a good neighborhood. The purpose of this little jaunt was to pick up an embroidered silk jacket for her mother, cornflower blue with little yellow petals on the sleeves. I discouraged her from going. I didn't understand why she was being so thoughtful to a woman who once dragged her across the floor by her ponytail." Trish was glad to hear gasps from the crowd as Honey's eyes blazed. "I guess Lorelei was a better person than me because I don't forgive easily, and she forgave everyone." Trish took a long deep breath in preparation for the piece-de-resistance. "It's ironic that the mother she forgave for years of cruelty was the cause of her death. If Honey hadn't had a birthday in July, Loree wouldn't have been at that particular place at that particular time."

Honey seethed; the rage was almost visible, like steam. Aaron had to restrain her from rushing to the podium.

The murmuring in the chapel bubbled up, but this time with a potent undercurrent. The possibility of ambush percolated in Trish's head, and she realized she was ill-prepared for any kind of physical attack; her dress was lightweight, the shoes all wrong. Instead of returning to her seat, she took the express route to the nearest exit door.

The sun managed to surface and beat down on Trish like a follow spot. Trish (or Trash, as she began to refer to herself) scurried to her rental car, jumped in and promptly locked the door. She considered waiting for Jesse and whisking him off to some out-of-the-way spot for a quickie, but she didn't want to tempt karma.

Lazy, listless and fifty-eight, Trish's parents hadn't changed in any discernible way since the last time she saw them. Her rail-thin mother, Irene, continued to look at the world through gauze thanks to her six-tranquilizers-a-day habit. Norm may have lost a couple of pounds, but he still wasted his time with his two favorite activities: drinking and sitting, both of which he could do while yelling at ball games on TV.

Everything, every habit, every secret, every detail, came flooding back. Trish remembered exactly where her mother hid her vials of pills – under the left seat cushion of the sofa. She recalled her method of gauging her father's level of intoxication when he got home from work – by the number of seconds it took him to get his key in the front door. The runaway daughter was back, knee-deep in a molasses-thick silence. The parents still seemed content with their routine, walking around in what Trish referred to as a London Fog.

Within Trish's reach were a host of amenities – her old bedroom, a refrigerator filled with food, a hammock in the back yard – but she rejected them. It felt wrong to succumb to the slightest bit of physical comfort in such an emotionally dusty environment. Not a single item was new. From the dishes to the towels to the dusty books on the shelves to the Kellogg's Raisin Bran Crunch in the kitchen cabinet, everything was exactly as it had been for twenty years.

Remote in hand, Irene channel-surfed. "There it is," she said. "Have you ever seen this?" It was some reality show involving ordinary people given fashion makeovers.

"Nope," Trish told her. "I don't watch much TV."

Irene was instantly fascinated by a bovine grandmother in a floral muumuu, her hair a frantic rat's nest. "I can't wait to see what she looks like *after*," Irene said with as much excitement as Trish had seen in her in sixteen years. Norm's head was leaning back on his armchair, his heavy eyelids losing their battle to stay open. Trish wondered how things might have been if her brother hadn't died young and her parents hadn't permanently retreated into a state of shock.

Even after sixteen years, Roger was present in every room of the house. His personal belongings were displayed on shelves, museum-style, with an index card explaining the significance of each: his baseball mitt, a bowling trophy, a silver watch, his football, a pair of weather-beaten black boots. Roger was the undisputed hero of the house, and his remnants were more alive than the human inhabitants.

"I'll bet they color her hair a kind of ash blonde," Irene mumbled, eyes still glued to the screen.

The irony was disturbing to Trish. Her mother was mesmerized by a show in which women were given makeovers while she barely noticed the major physical transformation her own daughter had made. It maddened Trish that neither parent asked about Lorelei's funeral or life in New York or anything that mattered. Teetering between driving to the airport for the first flight anywhere else and strangling both parents with her bare hands, Trish was about to burst. "Why didn't you go to Loree's funeral?" she blurted at her mother.

"Just a minute," Irene whispered. "Commercial break."

Trish repeated the question. Taken aback, her mother looked away from the TV but not at Trish. "We hardly knew her," she sighed, staring at the carpet. "You always went over to her house, remember? She never came over here. Besides, I don't care for her mother."

"*Nobody* cares for her mother but that didn't stop them from showing up."

"I don't even own a black dress."

"Gray would have been fine."

"With sequins? All I have is the one I wore to your cousin Sissy's wedding."

The commercial break was over and Irene's eyes were back on the small screen. Trish felt like she was onstage in a very depressing, badly written, poorly acted play. She could tell that the restless audience was counting the minutes until the curtain call. "I'm going for a drive," she announced. She grabbed her bag and marched out of the house.

Escaping was an easy out, and Trish had done it before. Ostensibly it was her parents who she was running from, but she wondered if she would ever land in a destination that would satisfy her. Or would there always be some better place in her mind, a utopia where she would find like-minded people also running toward some imaginary someplace?

Everything she passed had an estranged familiarity – ramshackle houses, the 7-Eleven, the corner diner known for its biscuits and gravy, the Texaco gas station where her mother accidentally left her behind when she was seven, the baseball field where Roger hit a game-winning home run. Trish began to feel trapped, as she always had growing up. She made a sudden turn.

Lorelei's house, though only two miles from Trish's, was in a much ritzier zip code. Not exactly 90210, but the properties were more impressive and the lawns large and immaculate. As she turned onto Mulligan Place, Trish was smacked with an instant surge of emotion, primal fear mixed with mournful gloom. This was the first time she'd ever been on this street without her best friend.

The sun was setting; hot pink streaks slashed across a violet sky. The humid air was uncomfortably still. Not the slightest breeze blew through the old willow tree on Lorelei's front lawn. This was *their* tree. On Sunday afternoons, the girls would stretch out under it on nylon lawn chairs or chaise lounges, gabbing about school activities, cute boys, lip gloss, older boys, fashion, boys they wished weren't gay, teachers they thought were most likely to molest a student, and how they never wanted to become their parents. This was their haven, sacred ground. Nothing could hurt them under the old weeping willow.

The Frick driveway was jammed with cars. Trish stepped out of the rental, banged the door closed, then changed her mind and opened it.

"Hey Trish! Is that you?" It was Jesse, emerging from the house, barefoot. "I was at the window and saw you pull up."

She turned and offered a weak smile. "Yep, it's me."

"You wanna come in?" he asked, quickly approaching.

"No, I think I'm going to head out."

"Then how about taking me for a drive?"

She hesitated. "Sure, why not?"

"Cool. Wait here for a sec? I just wanna run inside."

"All right."

"You won't leave without me?" he asked with a boyish grin.

"I won't leave. I promise."

He scooted off as Trish sank back into the driver's seat. She tried to rationalize her decision to wade in these potentially dangerous waters, telling herself she was bringing a little joy to a lonely, small town guy, though she didn't have the slightest evidence to suggest he was lonely. If nothing else, she'd get through the night with a fling and a prayer, and eventually the experience would become a bittersweet memory to recall with nostalgia and a laugh.

Jesse jumped into the passenger seat, excitement crackling through his agile body. Suddenly the fresh scent of Pepsodent permeated the entire front half of the vehicle. Trish found this endearing. "You smell so clean," she told him.

"Thanks. I showered after the funeral."

"I'm glad to hear it."

"Yeah, it's a good idea to uh...shower after a funeral," he stammered, "or any big event. Especially in this heat." His legs were almost too long to fit into the car, but he managed, and Trish started the engine.

Two hours later, after a leisurely stroll near the lake, banana splits at the Dairy Queen, and a half joint of White Widow, Trish and Jesse landed in the rental car, parked behind a cluster of trees. With light heads and busy hands, they leaned back on their individual seats. Trish's right hand played with the radio dials while Jesse's left massaged Trish's right leg. "Why is this area always so dark?" she asked.

"The lamp is busted."

"Did you bust it on purpose?"

"Yeah, just before you came I threw a cantaloupe at it," he said.

"Why can't I find a decent radio station?"

"Fuck the music," he said. "I don't need music. Just sit back and listen to the crickets."

"I miss the sound of crickets."

"I always had a crush on you, y'know," he confessed.

"Get out," she playfully said.

"No I really did. Remember the night you slept over?"

"I slept over lots of times."

"Yeah but there was only one when you and Lorelei fell asleep on the couch. Remember that?"

"I think I do actually. It was late and we were too tired to get up and go to the bedroom. We thought about calling a taxi."

"You were all covered up except one leg. One entire leg."

"Right or left?" she asked.

"Left. I stared at it for the longest time, maybe an hour. It was the most spectacular thing I'd ever seen, and it was just a few feet away from me."

"You were feet from my leg?"

"Almost close enough to touch."

"But you didn't."

"Almost. I put my hand real fucking close to it. The next morning you took a shower, and when you were finished I grabbed the towel you used. Kept it in my room for damn near a week."

"Wow," she sighed with wonder. "I don't want to know what you did with it."

"Then I won't tell you. Hey, you wanna fuck?"

"Huh? What? Here?"

"Unless you wanna do it in the house, but it's full of relatives. My cousin Davey's in my room."

"The funeral," she said. "Of course." Suddenly the mood turned somber. "Listen Jesse, there's something I want you to know."

"What?"

"Your sister was going to insist you move to New York."

Jesse was stunned. "No shit?"

"No shit. Would you have gone?"

"In a heartbeat. Anything to get out of this hellhole."

"Yeah, it's a pretty big hole with a whole lot of hell." Out of nowhere, Trish began to sob.

"Are you crying because you're happy?"

"No," she managed to say.

"Because you're turned on?"

She shook her head. "No."

"But you're definitely crying, right?"

"I'm crying because I can see my entire life ahead of me, and my best friend isn't there."

Though their hands were on each other's legs, they stopped moving. Trish and Jesse sat in comfortable silence.

"Wish you weren't leaving," he said. "Wish I could see you tomorrow and the next day."

"You can still come to New York," she responded.

"Really?"

"Sure. I'd help you get settled."

"I might take you up on it."

Trish saw the wheels turning in Jesse's head. "That's what Loree would've wanted. She felt guilty leaving you with your mother."

"That bitch was worse to Loree than she was to me."

"Look at me," Trish instructed softly. He stared with attentive eyes, and she held his gaze. "You'll think about New York, you'll decide to go, then you'll chicken out. But I want you to know the invitation will always be there, always, even a year from now. Or two, three years."

"Thanks," he said. Slowly they came together, lips electric. They sat in the car, in the dark, making out and stroking each other to the relaxing beat of the crickets.

"Trish fucking London," Jesse breathed.

"Jesse fucking Frick." With deep contentment, Trish smiled warmly, her hand on Jesse's jeans.

The Missing Bridesmaid

Three feet off the tile floor, Sherri Lambirth stood on an aluminum stepladder, struggling to reach a box of roofing nails for the highly disagreeable Lurene Crowley. Standing proudly, like a peacock showing off its plumage, Lurene was terribly taken with her new summer dress – a black and mauve monstrosity festooned with sparkling brooches, each in the shape of a butterfly or fish. With her recently colored hair verging on tangerine and her lipstick the shade of undercooked pork, she looked more like a travelling circus performer than a retired switchboard operator. Lurene was known for the three Rs: regifting, remarrying, and regurgitating after drinking too many rum toddies at local functions. "Do you think you'll find the nails before the New Year?" she asked in her Texas drawl. (She'd moved north a decade earlier because her fifth husband, Otis, hated the south's oppressive heat and ubiquitous "y'alls.") "Almost got it," Sherri chirped. Not even Lurene could pry the smile from her lips.

"Is this the box you want?" a male voice inquired, a large hand holding the thin package.

"The flat two-inchers, yes," she responded without turning her head. Once she stepped down from the ladder (with the support of that same hand), her eyes met those of Keelan Dunne, and she felt a physical jolt like a moderate earthquake. Heart raced, body temperature rose, arms went limp. "Hi," she breathed. With soulful blue eyes, soothing smile, and head of wavy blondish hair, the boy in front of her smoldered. Sherri felt the heat in the deepest part of her gut. Her hand gripped the ladder.

"Hi, I'm Keelan. It's Irish."

"I'm Sherri," she replied. "American."

"I'm Lurene," Mrs. Crowley reminded them from three feet away. "Customer."

"Oh sorry!" Sherri said. "Here are the roofing nails for Mr. Crowley to fix the uh…the.."

"Roof," Lurene barked, grabbing the box of nails from Sherri and brusquely marching away. But being the curious, cold-eyed observer of all things None of Her Business, she didn't march very far. Pretending to inspect light bulbs and extension cords, she remained close enough to eavesdrop on the conversation.

"Thanks for helping me," Sherri gushed to the stranger, scanning his square-jawed face. "I'd bet good money that you don't live nearby."

"You'd be a winner," he replied, receptive to her steady gaze. "Flew in from Omaha for my cousin's wedding."

"Your cousin wouldn't be Priscilla Wooten, would it?"

"It would," he answered, grinning.

"No way! I'm a bridesmaid!" Sherri squeaked, mentally noting never to allow her voice to reach that pitch again. "She's one of my best friends, but she never told me about an out-of-town cousin."

"I only met her one time," he admitted. "Her mom and my dad are brother and sister, but they were never close."

"That's too bad." A few seconds of silence passed as they marinated in the heat of their connection. "So what are you doing in the store?" Sherri asked.

"I came to buy a paring knife."

"Then follow me," Sherri instructed, buoyantly leading him down the aisle. Because of the ballet classes she took from age eight to thirteen, she moved with the grace of a dancer. Keelan, on the other hand, walked like a jock with big clumsy steps, his arms swinging loosely at his side.

In the middle of aisle six was a large display of knives. "This one's my favorite," Sherri told Keelan, scooping up a German-made piece of cutlery. "It has a five-inch blade with a removable mahogany handle, and it's perfect for peeling, mincing, carving radishes or de-veining shrimp."

"Cool." He smiled, focusing less on the knife than on Sherri's hazel eyes, glossy auburn hair, and upswept breasts. "I'll take it."

"My gift to you," she oozed. "For helping me reach the nails."

"Wow, thanks."

"Well, it only cost us fifty cents," she told him conspiratorially. "Just slip it in your pocket."

The fear of Keelan leaving the store brought a wave of panic in Sherri that was unfamiliar and alarming. She understood that nobody had ever taken hold of her nerves, her heart, her head, every part of her so overwhelmingly. All she could do was follow instructions she was getting from powers unknown. "I'm so in the mood for a mocha cappuccino," she blurted out.

"Then let's get one," he said. "Do you need to ask your boss?"

"He's my dad. This isn't a real job," she explained.

Sherri and Keelan dashed out the rear exit of Wade's Hardware and headed for the Starbucks a half-block west. The warm July air was drenched with gray gloom; the sun was trying to peek through the swirling clouds, to no avail. "How'd you get so tan?" Sherri asked, feasting her eyes on Keelan's sun-bronzed skin.

"I'm outside a lot," he responded, watching her walk, her legs and hips working together like well-oiled cogs.

"Me too, but I'm still white as a refrigerator. Look at *you*, though. The sun wrapped its rays around you and turned you golden."

"That's really poetic. Are you a writer?"

"No, I plan to make decent money," she replied, laughing. "I'm going to Brown in the fall."

"Brown," he repeated with a nod of his head, as if granting his approval. (He had no idea what Brown was.) After he paid for the drinks, Sherri led him past a row of shops and the town's only post office to a small park. Framed by well-tended evergreen shrubs and lavender lilac bushes, it was the ideal location for a romantic scene in a movie, soundtrack courtesy of a gurgling brook. Two giant maple trees towered overhead, their leaves swaying in the light breeze.

"I love this spot," Sherri sighed as she and Keelan sat down on a wrought iron bench with oak wood slats. "Sometimes I sit here with a book for hours. Because of the rain we get, the foliage is always growing. Look at all the shades of green. I can see forest green, sea green, pine, olive, even a little jade. Did you know it rains 250 days a year here? Sometimes it's just a drizzle, but it's still rain." She paused in horror. "Oh God, I'm babbling more than that brook. Please tell me to shut up."

"I *like* hearing you talk," he said. "Hey, you know the all-time best way to look at something that's beautiful?"

"No," she said, intrigued. "Tell me."

"Close your eyes and pretend you're dead. Then pretend you're given one final chance to come back and examine that beautiful thing. You open your eyes, and there it is."

"Fantastic," she marveled.

"That's the idea." He smiled, sliding a piece of gum in his mouth. After a few solid chews, Keelan reached over and kissed her gently. Within twenty seconds, the kiss had grown in intensity, and before

Sherri knew it, her back was horizontal on the hard wood bench. Blissfully comfortable under the considerable heft of Keelan's body, she wrapped her arms around him, allowing her hands to explore the curves of his back and butt. His tongue licked Sherri's lips, and she gasped, bucking her hips up to him as his fingers deftly slid under her shirt. Then he lifted himself off her and gazed into her eyes. "That was amazing," he said, his voice melodious.

"For me, too," she sighed dreamily. At this point, Sherri was convinced Keelan was the one to whom she wanted to hand her destiny. He made her feel safe enough to say anything, promise everything, and indulge in the kind of reckless, wild fantasies she'd never previously entertained. She wanted to undress him to Debussy's *Clair de Lune* and leave marks on his body. She wanted to attach herself to him like a conjoined twin. She wanted to use his ass as a pillow and sleep on it for nights on end. She wanted to have his body for breakfast, lunch, and dinner.

"What are you thinking?" he asked.

"Well," Sherri mused, hesitating only slightly. "I've never been with a guy all the way before, and I'd like you to be my first." Unlike her close friend and Keelan's cousin Priscilla, Sherri never harbored any illusions of waiting until marriage.

"Wow," Keelan said, excited, stunned and overwhelmed. "I uh... I'm only here till tomorrow."

"My dad always told me there's no time like the present."

"Not sure this is what he had in mind."

"I always followed the rules and never got into trouble," Sherri said. "Not even once. I've been saving up for the time when trouble would present itself, and here it is. Don't you think I paid my dues?"

"You're probably paid up through next spring," he agreed enthusiastically.

Fingers curling together like they couldn't get close enough,

Sherri led Keelan to the Red Roof Lodge, a ten-room motel owned and operated by the parents of her offbeat pal Brianna Rykoff. Her parents were on a ten-day vacation that took them to Versailles, Pamplona, and Kiev, which meant Brianna and her mischievous younger brother Meat (short for Dmitri) were running the place.

Sherri darted into the lobby and grabbed the key to room 9. "How long you want it for?" Brianna asked, barely taking her heavily mascaraed eyes off her toenails, which she was painting candy-apple red.

"The rest of my life," Sherri mumbled, barely audible.

Keelan followed her up one flight of carpeted stairs and then down a hallway of flickering fluorescents, anticipation building with every step. Their designated room had no charm, no character, and no bathtub. The art on the walls was unforgivable and the TV set wasn't even a flat-screen. The air was stale, as if the room had been unoccupied for weeks. But the queen-size bed was clean and cozy, and that was all that mattered. This was where Sherri and Keelan consummated their forty-minute long relationship. Keelan's large muscular frame melded beautifully with Sherri's bouncing young breasts, narrow waist, and long, slender legs. Sherri's tender white skin tingled with sublime pleasure, and she felt every cell in her body coddled and caressed. "I can't stop touching you," he whispered as she wrapped her legs around his waist.

"Don't," she moaned into his ear.

Afterwards, wrapped in a cloud of bliss, Sherri closed her eyes and embedded her head on Keelan's chest. "You feel so great," she sighed, out of her mind in love.

As the minutes crept by, thin beams of sunlight radiated through the two inches of window visible behind the blue curtains. The lovers cuddled and kissed, interspersing soft moments between multiple sessions of lovemaking. When they spooned, Keelan's breath was deliciously warm on the back of her neck. This was Sherri's new favorite place on the planet – beside Keelan Dunne in a queen-size bed. She was certain she'd love him at sixty, seventy and eighty, stripped of his youthful beauty but still possessing the mysterious spark that filled her.

Sherri was astounded by the suddenness with which love arrived. Keelan came along and claimed her, and willingly she went. It was as if she was about to take a photograph of her entire life using a wide-angle lens. Just when every element was perfectly arranged and clearly in focus – parents, friends, school, future – Keelan Dunne stepped in front of the camera, obliterating everything behind him. The picture became a portrait.

Via cell phone, Sherri told her mother Violet that she was spending the night with Brianna.

"Are you sure?" Violet asked. "Tomorrow's the wedding."

"I'm sure," she responded. "Really, truly, absolutely." Before the barrage of questions began, Sherri pretended she lost signal. It was the first time she had ever fibbed to her mother, but she felt no guilt. What she felt was fate pulling its strings with a sturdy, sure-handed inevitability, arranging everything rapidly and rightfully. "I want to *die* this way," she tenderly told Keelan while snuggling against the soft golden skin of his torso.

"Do you mean that?" he asked.

"Yes. Really, truly, absolutely," she murmured.

"You're sure?"

"I am so totally sure."

"All right." Keelan reached over to his blue jeans which were hanging over the wooden desk chair, grabbed the paring knife Sherri had given him, and stabbed her seven times. He closed his eyes and took several deep breaths, awkwardly rolling off the rumpled bed with a thump. After rinsing the blood off his hands, arms and face, he grabbed two pieces of Trident watermelon sugarless gum, tossed them in his mouth and chewed like there was no tomorrow or next week.

⊕

The next day, the wedding of Priscilla Wooten and Dean Ward proceeded without a hitch except for the fact that one of the bridesmaids didn't show up. Violet had called the police when she didn't surface that Sunday morning, but because of the call Sherri made the previous day, the authorities didn't take the disappearance too seriously; they assumed the young girl had gone off on some wild romantic adventure.

Brianna Rykoff had completely forgotten that her friend had taken a room key, so it wasn't until Monday when Mr. and Mrs. Rykoff flew in from the Ukraine that Sherri's nude body, with its seven stab wounds, was discovered in bed at the Red Roof Lodge. The officers assigned to the case agreed this was the most gruesome, horrifying crime scene in the history of their district.

Violet Lambirth, who resembled Sherri to such a degree that they'd often been mistaken for sisters, decided to bury her daughter in the bridesmaid dress she'd planned to wear to Priscilla's wedding. She thought it would be a tribute to the event Sherri had been so eager to attend. Luckily it was no bridesmaid monstrosity, even though the sleeves were a bit puffy for Violet's taste.

Traffic moved slowly in the torrential rain, but that didn't stop those who wanted to pay their last respects to Sherri Lambirth. The church overflowed with shell-shocked friends, tranquilized neighbors, and still-smitten teenage boys who wanted to get one final look at their elusive goddess in her permanent bed of pine, the second most expensive coffin in the casket catalogue.

The police began a massive investigation. Every day, some new development grabbed the headlines despite no solid leads. "All I saw was the back of a head," Brianna explained to the media, "and I've seen the backs of so many that I can't tell one from the other."

Wednesday at midnight, the main terminal at Sea-Tac Airport was predictably desolate. A few scattered airline personnel wandered about, but the day's flights had arrived and departed.

A middle-aged janitor was emptying the trash in one of the men's rooms when he noticed an unusual silver glow amidst the paper towels and discarded fast food wrappers that filled the large plastic bag. With gloved hands, he took a closer look. It was the five-inch blade of a knife. Ordinarily, he would've tossed the item away, but because of the recent stabbing, he turned it into the police.

It was rapidly determined that this was the weapon that penetrated Sherri Lambirth's body seven times. (The mahogany handle that was attached to the blade had been removed.) A shocking revelation: the knife was traced to Wade's Hardware. Wade instantly removed the item from his shelves.

Violet Lambirth lay in her mess of a bed in a thick haze. With the curtains drawn and the lights dim, she'd retreated into a state of oblivion. Brushing her teeth, washing her hands, eating, working part-time at the hospital, even the simple act of getting dressed, no longer mattered. The spirit had been squeezed from her like water from a sponge, leaving nothing but crippling, inconsolable sadness.

The landline in Violet's bedroom blasted like a fire alarm, and she covered her ears. By the seventh sadistic ring, it seemed like the caller wasn't planning on giving up. Violet reluctantly reached over. "Hello," she croaked.

"This is Lurene Crowley, the gal who hit your Buick in the mall parking lot last year, remember? Red hair? Slim? Well-dressed?"

"What can I do for you, Lurene?" Violet asked, struggling to sit up in bed, pushing a box of tissues and a *TV Guide* to the floor.

"I know who killed your daughter," she bluntly said. "I saw him at your husband's hardware store."

Violet's heart began to race and the muscles in her body tightened. "You did?" she asked, gripping her pillow for support.

"Indeed I did. I didn't even hear about it till this morning. Otis and I were in Phoenix for the second wedding of my third husband's sister Sydelle. We got back today and I read about your girl. My heart's aching for you."

"Nice of you to say."

"I always suspected you were a decent person," Lurene explained, "even after making such a fuss about that little ding."

"Little ding?" Violet asked, bristling. "The entire door on the passenger side had to be replaced."

"I apologized, didn't I?"

"Tell me what you know about my daughter or I'll have a SWAT team banging on your door in five minutes."

"No need to get testy, sweets," Lurene said with only a smidgeon of fear. Then she recounted the story from the beginning, beginning with Sherri helping her find a box of roofing nails.

"You'd never seen him before?" Violet asked.

"No. He flew in for Dolores Wooten's daughter's wedding."

"How do you know all this?"

"I happened to be shopping for a box of roofing nails, and I couldn't help hearing part of their conversation."

"Listen to me," Violet said, eyes blazing. "As soon as you hang up the phone, you have to call the police station and ask for Officer Flanagan, he's leading the investigation. Tell him exactly what you just told me."

"I'll do that *pronto.*"

On the front page of all the morning newspapers was a photograph of Keelan Dunne looking GQ-handsome in his white shirt, silver tie and navy blue pinstripe suit.

The headline read: "STATE'S MOST WANTED MAN."

"I want to meet him," Violet told Officer Flanagan after Keelan was transported back to Tacoma and put behind bars.

It wasn't customary for a mother to want to meet her daughter's alleged killer, and Violet's request was summarily denied. After threatening to go to the press, .

Flanagan caved. "You can meet him," he told her on the telephone, "with one stipulation. The boy's parents want to meet you first."

"Why?" she asked with suspicion.

"I don't really know," he replied.

Violet didn't expect to like the parents of her daughter's murderer, assuming they'd failed miserably in the Raising Children Department. But the moment she laid eyes on them, all preconceived opinions vanished. Standing nervously side by side, their faces crumbling with anguish, Bernadette Dunne offered her quivering hand. "We're so very sorry," she said in a careful voice.

"We can't even put it into words," Jay Dunne added, holding out his hand in midair. "There just aren't words to express our sorrow."

The tense, tough expression on Violet's face softened. "Why did you want to talk to me?" she asked.

"Can we sit?" Bernadette inquired.

They moved to a secluded corner of the lobby. "You need to know a few things about our son," Jay said.

"And we want you to hear it from *us*," Bernadette added.

Violet shifted restlessly on the lumpy sofa. "I'm listening," she said.

It was Bernadette who told the story, starting with Keelan's odd behavior when he was three. After numerous visits to doctors, neurologists and psych wards, the young boy was diagnosed with autism. As he grew older, he seemed to mature normally. But around the age of ten, he became painfully shy and extremely awkward in social situations. He had no friends and dreaded going to school. He acted strangely and took things literally; he couldn't tell when someone was joking. His diagnosis was changed to Asperger Syndrome, a form of autism.

"When he turned fifteen," Jay interjected, "he had a growth spurt, physically. He developed into this great-looking young man, and he started getting all this attention. That's when we thought it was best to enroll him in a special school."

"He still goes there," Bernadette said. "He's very well-liked." Tears arrived suddenly; she angrily wiped them away.

The metal door opened slowly and silently. Violet braced herself, then carefully stepped into the sparse, refrigerated room, leaving two armed security guards standing outside. She deliberately averted her eyes from the man sitting on the other side of the enormous wooden table. As the door closed, Keelan gasped; that's when Violet forced herself to face him.

Keelan's mouth was hanging open and his eyes were bulging.

"Am I dreaming?" he asked. "Sherri? You look...you look exactly like Sherri."

Violet gingerly sat down and studied Keelan's face under the muted light. His eyes weren't the least bit elusive, the way she expected them to be. They were open, welcoming. He had a sculpted nose and the bronzed skin of a South Beach lifeguard. "You aren't dreaming," she said in a low voice, noticing that his hands were restrained in metal cuffs. "And I'm not Sherri." The insulated room, with its ratty brown carpet and stark white walls, had a coldness to it, literally and figuratively. "Why is it freezing enough to hang meat in here?"

"You even *sound* like her," Keelan said. "I can't believe it. You're Sherri."

"No," Violet calmly explained. "I'm the woman who *gave birth* to Sherri. I was very young at the time, barely eighteen." She shook her head, trying to banish memories of a quick marriage to man she wasn't sure she loved. "Sherri didn't *live* to eighteen." Now, faced with her daughter's murderer in this secluded room, the rage Violet expected to feel was surprisingly gone. "Will you answer my questions?" she asked, resting her shaky hands on the smooth brown surface of the table.

"Sure," he said. "I'll tell you anything. Everything. Whatever you want to know."

Violet believed him. "What did my daughter feel toward you?"

"Feel toward me," he murmured. His sorrowful eyes seemed to be travelling back in time, searching for honest answers. "We loved each other."

Violet was taken aback. "In the short time you spent together, you fell in love?"

"If you want to call it that." He closed his eyes and stroked

"What do *you* want to call it?"

He paused for a moment. "I guess love's the closest thing," he said, knowing that the profound feelings they had for each other were ineffable. Still, he tried to paint the picture. "We didn't fall in love. We fell into each other. We became part of each other."

Violet eyed him with suspicion. "Tell me what it felt like," she said.

"It was magical," he said, shutting his eyes. "It felt like we could accomplish anything. As long as we were together, it felt like we could *fly* if we wanted to."

"Very poetic. Please open your eyes and look at me."

"*Sherri* was the poetic one," Keelan said, opening his eyes. "Not me."

"Yes, she *was* poetic. How many stabs did it take to kill my daughter?" Violet asked in a detached, emotionless manner. "All seven?"

Shaken by the question, Keelan avoided looking at Violet, staring at the cuffed hands on his lap instead. "I don't know," he said.

Despite the cold air, sweat was gathering on Violet's forehead. She lifted one of her jittery hands from the table and wiped it away. "How could you not know, Keelan? Think back."

"My eyes were closed," he said. A tense pause followed. "It might've been after the second or maybe the third."

"Then why did you keep going? Why did you continue stabbing her?"

"I wanted to make sure I did the job all the way. I didn't want her to turn into some kind of vegetable."

"That was thoughtful," Violet said, her expression tightening. She took a deep, much needed breath. "Did she scream?"

"No," he said. "She trusted me, no matter what I did, just like I trusted her."

"If you loved her, why did you use the knife in the first place?"

"Because I thought she wanted me to," he said with sincerity.

Violet's head jerked back in disbelief. This was one scenario that hadn't even crossed her mind, and she thought she'd come up with every possibility in the book.

"Why on earth did you think she wanted you to?" she asked.

"We were in each other's arms, and she said 'I want to die like this.' That's what she said. I asked if she was sure, and she said yes. Well, what she *actually* said was, 'Really, truly, absolutely.' So I thought she wanted to die right then and there because that's what she said. I swear she said that. But now..well, now after what people told me, I'm not sure."

"You're not sure?" Violet asked.

"No," it pained him to say. "Not entirely."

"Not entirely sure," Violet slowly repeated as if she couldn't believe what she was hearing. "Didn't anyone explain this to you?"

Keelan looked lost and frightened, like a five-year-old separated from his mother in a crowded mall. "No," he mumbled. "All they told me was that she didn't really want to die even though she *said* she did."

"My God," Violet whispered in astonishment, staggered by the simplicity of Keelan's psyche. "You need to listen to what I'm going to tell you. Will you listen carefully?"

"Yes, I promise."

She took a few highly charged moments to gather her thoughts before speaking. "Sherri wasn't being realistic," Violet explained. "When she told you she wanted to die like that, she meant she wanted to be at your side when she was very old and *ready* to die. She meant that she wanted to spend her life with you, until the end. *That's* what she meant when she said, 'I want to die like this.'"

Keelan allowed the words to sink in. Gradually his face contorted into pieces. Tears were coming down his cheeks heavier than the rain outside. He tried to wipe them away, but it wasn't easy in handcuffs. His head suddenly jerked from left to right to left to right to left to right to left to right. Even after his neck went limp like the broken stem of a flower, the head continued to move vehemently, from left to right to left to right to left to right, as if trying to separate itself from the rest of his body. It wouldn't have surprised Violet to see him tearing at his own flesh.

It was clear to Violet that nobody fully understood the mysterious terrain of Keelan Dunne's head, its unending limitations, its childlike innocence and its fervent desire to do the proper thing. When he ended Sherri Lambirth's life, there was madness to his method. No evil, no malice. Just plain, old-fashioned madness.

Violet rose to her feet and slowly stepped toward him. She tenderly touched his head so that it would stop moving so violently, and it responded by slowing down before coming to a complete stop.

Violet leaned against the table. Her two hands gravitated to Keelan's head and held it like a precious gem. Then she carefully guided it to her chest. "She really captured your heart," Violet sadly said.

"Forever," he responded. A speck of colorful memory came alive in his head. Then it disappeared.

"And you captured *hers*." Keelan's physical closeness to Violet nourished, energized, and unnerved her. Appalled and embarrassed by this sudden surge of feeling, she closed her eyes. The mother was now standing in her dead daughter's shoes, carrying on something that seemed destined, preordained. Violet knew that this fleeting moment wouldn't last long enough; even if it lasted all day, the end would come too soon.

"Will I go to prison for the rest of my life?" Keelan quietly asked.

"No," she replied, opening her eyes. "I won't let that happen." She clenched a handful of his warm, silky hair, brought her lips to it, and allowed its fresh, masculine scent to penetrate her. "I feel her in your hair, on your skin. I see her in your eyes." The room was no longer cold.

Keelan's left cheek was now pressed against the bare skin of Violet's neck. "I love you so much," he whispered, holding onto her like he never wanted to let go, the idea of a second chance buried so deeply in the far reaches of his brain that he was only dimly aware of it. His head remained perfectly still.

"I love you, too," she whispered.

"What am I going to do?" he moaned. Keelan held on and couldn't help thinking what he didn't dare say out loud – that he wanted to die this way.

The ticking of the stainless steel clock on the wall sounded amplified. "Don't worry," Violet tenderly told him. "I'll take care of you."

Violet's hands crept down Keelan's scalp slowly, methodically, until they reached the neck with its baby soft, malleable skin. Her fingers formed a complete circle around his throat.

The clock kept ticking, louder and louder.

And Then There Was Scent

(This story contains 5% fact.)

THE BLAZING SUN BAKED the cement and scorched the grass until sidewalks and lawns became too hot to accommodate the soles of bare feet. July 1887, the hottest month ever for the city of Philadelphia, produced record highs and endless puddles, rivers and oceans of sweat. The temperature refused to go down with the sun; nights were often steamier than the days. For the first time in ecclesiastical history, nuns were granted special permission from the Vatican to remove the black veils and white headpieces of their habits while outdoors.

The heat was headline news across the country. The first half of July saw forty deaths from dehydration. In a bizarre coincidence, all forty victims were forty years of age.

Although people were repeatedly warned by the mayor to stay out of the sun, nineteen died of sunstroke during the second half of the month. In another strange coincidence, eighteen of the nineteen fatalities were fathers of eighteen-year-olds. The nineteenth was a fair-skinned, eighteen-year-old redhead with a constellation of freckles. She fell asleep on her chaise lounge under the influence of five bottles of beer and a small cheesecake.

Typical summer smells took on a malignant new life in the oppressive heat. Pedestrians passed out from the stench of garbage in the gutter and rotting leftovers in Dumpsters. Hopscotch was put on hold. Tag, tetherball, and Red Rover were banned due to the harsh body odor they produced.

Dr. Grover Beveridge, a renowned scientist of elephantine girth, excreted a potent odor from the exposure of all four hundred pounds of him to the heat. Colleagues resorted to holding garlic cloves to their noses to keep from fainting. They would have held flowers instead, had most not withered in the blistering heat.

In addition to being a scientist, Beveridge was a savvy attorney and businessman who understood the concept of supply and demand better than just about anyone; that's what made him a senior partner in the law firm of Wade Beveridge Wong Hedges Hathaway & Davies. During the heat wave, the rotund genius recognized a desperate demand, and he took it upon himself to find a solution to the body odor problem paralyzing his beloved hometown.

Beveridge practically *lived* in his laboratory, working tirelessly, ordering platters of cold cuts and kegs of raspberry lemonade, and experimenting with every odor-reducing substance known to science. After a period of trial and error, success was at hand! Thanks to a perfect combination of chemicals with a zinc compound as its base, a revolutionary product was born. It was called Mum, the very first underarm deodorant in cream form. It smelled like daisies.

Mum became a runaway sensation, as necessary to a morning routine as soap. Shop owners couldn't keep the product on the shelves. Now, thanks to Dr. Beveridge, there was no excuse for anyone to smell like a sewer.

Some creative women used Mum in unorthodox ways, like dabbing the cream on menstrual pads to reduce the chafing of the gauze. This brought comfort along with a lovely fragrance. Others, if seeking revenge on a roving, cheating husband, mixed the cream into the frosting of a cake, causing cramps, constipation, and dramatic Tourette's-like seizures. This was not what Dr. Beveridge had in mind, and it inspired him to add a warning to the label of each jar: *Only use as directed.*

After landing a lucrative book deal with Knickerbocker Press (later to become G. P. Putnam's Sons), Beveridge knocked out a candid, revealing memoir. *The Smell of Me* topped the bestseller list for an astonishing, record-shattering one hundred weeks. He was also named the wealthiest overweight man in the state. Women threw themselves at the obese billionaire, and he ended up marrying some of Philadelphia's most scintillating bombshells, including Priscilla Slate, a popular fan dancer who spent most of her time naked behind ostrich feathers.

After his seventh divorce in five years, Beveridge was convinced by his publisher to write a follow-up to the memoir, and he completed it in record time. *All Women Are Gold-Digging Sluts* didn't achieve the runaway success of *The Smell of Me*, though it garnered rave reviews. Thomas Genoways of the *New York Tribune* wrote: "I was afraid this would be an arch exercise in the cloying metaphysics of romantic irony, but Beveridge's latest reminded me of Goethe's *Sorrows of Young Werther*. He avoids shopworn topics, post-hoc sophistry and false dichotomies, choosing instead to explore the elusive line between opportunism and true partnership, and he does so with the ease of a master essayist."

William R. Quay of the *Pittsburgh Post-Gazette* put forth the following: "The author's style is immensely intriguing, especially when profiling the women who shared his custom-designed bed, reportedly the size of a small playground. The passages about his first wife, Nola Van Nostrand, are poetry dipped in vitriol. But he saves the best for his last spouse, the enigmatic Yvonne Marmaro. Like a pointillist painter, Beveridge supplies us with vivid dots of Yvonne, and it's up to the reader to connect them into a coherent portrait of an incoherent, insatiable, money-hungry hussy who can see no further than her tongue can reach."

Despite the unanimous critical acclaim, book sales were tepid. The popularity of Mum, however, continued to grow as rapidly as its creator's waistline. After adding a hundred pounds to his gargantuan frame, Beveridge could no longer climb out of his custom-made bed unassisted. In 1894, just seven years after introducing Mum to the world, Grover Beveridge died. The official cause of death was obesity, but several renowned doctors believed Beveridge's death was a direct result of a dairy overdose.   (He had recently attended Pennsylvania's Annual Butter, Milk, and Buttermilk Festival.)

With the exception of the devastating stock market crash, two bloody world wars and the "Fatty" Arbuckle scandal, the years between 1894 and 1950 rolled by smoothly. Mum continued to keep human bodies odor-free, and by the mid 1950s, a young dynamo named Helen Barnett Diserens had joined the production team. One of only two female chemistry majors who graduated from the University of Michigan, Helen hopped a train to New York to pursue the kind of electrifying life the Midwest couldn't offer. As the train roared east, her excitement built to such a fever pitch that she had to be sedated.

The enterprising young lady landed a job with Bristol-Myers and was assigned to the Mum account. Inspired by a popular new item on the market called the ballpoint pen, the ingenious chemist came up with a different method of applying deodorant: rolling it on. Instead of repackaging Mum, an entire new product was created: Ban Roll-On.

Even in a pre-internet universe, it didn't take long for such an important development to find a place on the world stage. That same day, newspapers around the globe carried the story. From the front page of a popular German publication: *ist ein Korperpflegemittel, das vorwiegend in den Achselhöhlen aufgebracht wird, um unangenehmen Korpergeruch zu bekämpfen, Ban Roll-On.*

The earth was a better smelling planet.

THE FACTS:

- Mum was created in 1888 by an inventor in Philadelphia whose name has been lost to history.

- Some women really used Mum on menstrual pads to reduce the chafing of the gauze that usually covered them.

- Helen Barnes Diserens was an actual person, now deceased, who worked for Bristol-Myers. Inspired by the ballpoint pen, she created Ban Roll-On.

Gone Shopping

WITH A THERMOMETER JUTTING from his pursed lips, Matthew Bochner was sitting up in a bed spotted with tissues. Carolyn knocked twice on the half open door. "Busy?"

"Just taking my temperature." Matthew sounded like he had a mouth full of food.

Carolyn pushed open the door and entered the dimly-lit room. She watched Matthew as he removed the thermometer from his mouth and struggled to make out his current temperature. "How can you see anything in here?" she asked. "It's darker than an Abercrombie & Fitch store." She pulled back a curtain and opened a window, to a waft of cool air and a brilliant panel of sunlight.

"That's better," Matthew admitted, eyes still on the thermometer. A few seconds later, he lifted himself off the bed, wobbling like a newborn colt. Holding the thermometer aloft like a trophy, he exclaimed, "99!"

"Congratulations," Carolyn exclaimed with glee. This was major news.

The night-table to the right of the bed was heaped with vials of prescription medication; at least a dozen bottles surrounded the silver lamp. The table to the left held a plastic, twelve-compartment pill organizer packed with colorful capsules like peanut M & Ms. Next to it was a ceramic cereal bowl brimming with red and white tablets. An inhaler, nebulizer and peak flow meter were stashed behind the bowl.

"You look good today," Carolyn announced, grinning.

"I *feel* good, but I look like I've been on a hunger strike since 2008."

"No," she assured him. "Maybe December '09."

"If I were any skinnier, I'd be a voice."

She gave him a slow, amused smile. "Do you know how many runway models would *kill* to be this thin?"

"It used to be called the heroin chic look. Will you go shopping with me?" he asked. "I'm tired of being cooped up in this room and I might not be around next month, my love."

Carolyn's had stopped telling her brother-in-law that he had countless days ahead of him and his future was bright and cheery. She'd made a promise to him: no more polite lies. No more false hope. "Sure," she answered. "Let's go shopping."

It took Matthew fifteen minutes to change into proper clothes for his first public outing in over a week. His muscles, joints, and bones moved sluggishly, and Carolyn had to assist him each step of the way. His ribs protruded, his legs were more bone than flesh. It was a body seized by illness again, abducted during the night when no one was watching. Still, Matthew had been a beautiful, blue-eyed, brown-haired young man, and traces of his attractiveness lingered, albeit subtly, on his still-boyish face.

Everything was big on him: jeans, shirt, crew-neck cashmere sweater. The last hole on his leather belt was too long by inches, so Carolyn punched a new hole in it with a pair of scissors. "See? We can solve any wardrobe malfunction," she boasted. Struck by the sight of this frail forty-year-old standing before her, half smiling, shoulders hunched, she gently put her arms around him. She could've wrapped her arms around him twice.

Matthew had been living in the Noe Valley section of San Francisco when he got sick. Andy Grant, his partner of three years, had been taking care of him until he took a severe turn for the worse. Matthew didn't leave his heart in the city by the bay, only some clothes that no longer fit and a few pieces of art he didn't want to schlep with him. Andy had a new boyfriend, and Matthew had grown disgruntled with the steep hills and gloomy weather.

"What did I do to deserve you?" Matthew asked, happy to feel human touch for a purpose other than taking his blood pressure.

"Well, somewhere in your youth or childhood, you must've done something good."

"I guess so."

Matthew and Carolyn shared a level of comfort rarely found between any two people. Her mere presence revved him up. It was an established fact that they had more in common with each other than she did with Matthew's older brother, Wayne, the dolt who happened to be her husband. Not that she didn't love the guy, but their interests were art museums and football fields apart. Like Matthew, Carolyn had a keen appreciation for jazz, literature, and Broadway musicals. *Unlike* Matthew, she appeared healthy and robust.

It had been Carolyn's idea for Matthew to move back into the eight thousand square foot family home on Sycamore Drive in Hancock Park, the kind of place where streets named after trees still had trees. From the outside, the Bochner house, stately and colonial with its white columns and perfectly-manicured lawns, resembled a museum. Despite its pretentious grandeur, Matthew was woven so deeply into this structure of his childhood – its spacious rooms, old-fashioned furniture – that coming back felt like falling into the comforting arms of a trusted friend.

"What do you want to shop for?" Carolyn asked, thinking bedding or books.

In a conspiratorial tone Matthew whispered, "An urn. For my ashes. I've earned the right to choose my own urn, don't you think?"

Carolyn fell silent. The shock of the request hit her like a boulder. It was one thing to be honest with Matthew about his declining health; it was another to help him choose an urn. "Uh, sure," she finally responded. "I do think you've earned that right."

"You're uncomfortable."

"Not really." She paused. "Maybe a little."

"No," he said. "A lot."

"OK, I'm uncomfortable," she admitted. "So what? I'll get over it."

"You don't have to go with me, Carolyn."

"I don't want you to go by yourself," she stated firmly. "You wouldn't let me go by myself."

"No I wouldn't."

"Then we're going. Together. Let's hit the road."

"Where's Wayne?" Mathew asked.

"Last I checked he was shooting baskets in the back yard."

"Of course. Where else would he be, in the den reading Descartes?"

Carolyn grinned. "You want him to come with us?"

"God no!" Matthew gasped.

"I didn't think so."

They headed down the hall to find Wayne, in a rumpled T-shirt and shorts, popping the tab on a can of Pepsi in the kitchen. His cheeks were pink and robust. He was more than a little overweight. Matthew sighed as he pulled himself into the kitchen.

"We're going out," Carolyn announced.

"Out?" he asked incredulously. "You really want people to see you, Matthew?"

"He feels good today."

"What about how he *looks?* If I was that skinny I'd stay behind closed doors and heavy curtains."

"Well, you're *not* this skinny," Matthew said. "You're actually kind of pudgy, so if I were *you*, I'd stay behind closed doors and live off Daddy's money. Oh. I forgot, that's what you're doing."

"Fuck you."

Carolyn stifled a laugh. "Are you both six years old?" She grabbed Matthew's hand and led him into the cool September afternoon.

Matthew's humble demeanor clashed with his older brother's volcanic sense of entitlement. Even as children they were polar opposites. Matthew followed the rules and Wayne broke them. Matthew studied diligently and Wayne cut classes to get high in the bathroom. At sixteen, Wayne took his father's Bentley and rammed it into a mailbox. As punishment, he was forced to stay home the next day and rake leaves while Matthew was taken sailing. He'd never gotten over it.

"What did you ever see in him?" Matthew asked as he hobbled to the green Honda in the gravel driveway.

"I love him, but sometimes I don't like him very much."

"He's a lazy, immature son-of-a-bitch with a chip on his shoulder. You deserve better, Carolyn."

"So where's the nearest Urns-R-Us?" she asked, changing the subject, mostly because she shared Matthew's opinions.

"If I'm not mistaken, and I rarely am, there's a big pottery store on Robertson that has a whole urn section. And if anyone asks, I'm on a starvation diet for a role in a new Holocaust movie."

"Brilliant," she laughed.

The pottery shop was located in one of the most bustling commercial areas of the city, on the border of Beverly Hills where every parking spot sparkled with Jaguars, BMWs, and the occasional Corniche. They gravitated toward the back, where Matthew cradled an urn with a tasteful black and gold pattern. "You think I'd look good in this?" he asked.

"No," Carolyn responded frankly. "I see you in blue." Her taste was always impeccable.

"You're so right. Blue is a good color for me. How's *this* one?" he asked, pointing to a turquoise urn with a white dove painted on it.

"Do you really want to spend eternity in turquoise? I was thinking more of a cobalt blue or a cerulean." Matthew nodded in hearty agreement.

"You like those rustic antique ones?" he asked, pointing to a row toward the bottom.

"I prefer the cultured marble. They seem more solid."

"Yeah, I do too. In fact, I like this bright one."

Carolyn picked it up with curiosity. "Not bad," she murmured, "but I don't think you want your final resting place to be called Dandelion Delight, do you?"

Further down the aisle, their eyes fell upon the perfect urn. Porcelain. Azure.

No silly patterns. Both stopped in their tracks as if having discovered a long lost treasure. "This is it," Carolyn announced.

Matthew reached for the urn, cradled it like a newborn. "Gorgeous," he breathed.

"Are you sure this is the one?" Carolyn asked. But she already knew.

"No question."

"Agreed. Let's get it."

The moment they arrived home, Matthew carried the urn to his bedroom while Carolyn poured herself a glass of cranberry juice in the kitchen. Still standing at the open refrigerator, she took one giant gulp after another, as if her thirst would never be fully quenched. Then she stepped to the counter and leaned against it, released the strain of holding herself up. She closed her eyes and wept.

Eleven months after the afternoon shopping spree, the divorce of Carolyn and Wayne Bochner was final. She asked for nothing of monetary value. All she wanted was the urn that held Matthew's ashes.

Wayne honored her request. He didn't care for the color anyway.

Whites in Hot Water

Her husband's white cotton T-shirt, resting in the dryer, reminded Maggie Skillet of a fluffy vanilla soufflé. She stared with awe, as if looking at her first full moon.

"You've got to see this!" she shouted to Roy. "Right now!"

Roy dragged his eyes away from his BlackBerry, rose from the sofa on which he was slouched, and hauled himself to his wife, who was kneeling in front of the energy-efficient dryer in the laundry room, its glass-front door opened. "Your T-shirt," she said in a gentle voice. "It looks like a piping-hot soufflé, don't you think?"

"Looks more like a T-shirt," he responded before strolling back to the living room. The notion of comparing a shirt to a dessert was as asinine to him as Maggie seeing a similarity between a blue flannel bed sheet and the Yakima River at dusk, which had happened the night before.

Maggie stood up, grabbed the crew neck T-shirt from the dryer and folded it with the precision of a seasoned salesperson, and then the two white hand towels, two pairs of white socks, and the white boxer briefs Roy seldom wore because they were snug (His waist had expanded two inches in six months). By conventional standards, it was a meager load of laundry, but Maggie's loads had become smaller and smaller as the frequency with which she washed clothing had increased.

Having her own washing machine and dryer was more than a mere luxury to Maggie Skillet; it was an incomparable thrill. As a little girl, she and her mother would trek seven blocks to the Laundromat, each carrying a load in a pillowcase. It was like going to the circus. When Maggie went away to Seattle University, the laundry room was in the basement of her dormitory building. Since she suffered from claustrophobia, she avoided the tiny, dimly-lit elevator and five-flight descent, opting to struggle down the well-lit stairs with a full basket of dirty clothes in her arms.

One Thanksgiving, Maggie's college roommate and best friend Allison Husk invited her to her family's estate in Savannah. It wasn't the majestic white stone columns on the front porch, or the Steinway parlor grand piano in the living room, or the William and Mary-style armoires in each bedroom that impressed Maggie; it was the laundry room. She had never been in a house with its own laundry facilities, and she couldn't help gawking at the washer/dryer combo as if it were made of pure platinum.

Maggie made it through four years of marriage without comparing a single freshly laundered item to anything edible, no green sock spinach leaves, no red blouse raspberry sorbets. But on a rainy Sunday morning shortly after their fifth anniversary, Maggie's imagination took flight. She proclaimed a burnt umber bath towel, just removed from the dryer, a perfect semblance of a pan of fudge brownies straight from the oven. "Don't you think so?" she asked Roy.

"Maybe if you're on some kind of hallucinogen," he replied. These occasional comparisons, though bizarre, didn't bother Roy in any significant way. He dismissed them as another of his wife's offbeat spurts, like the quilting, candle-making, or balloon animals, all of which entertained her for a short time, then vanished for good.

Green-eyed Maggie Gallagher had grown up to be a wavy-haired, willowy woman with quirky sensibilities, few friends, and a plethora of poetry anthologies. She never loved Roy Skillet in a magical, all-consuming way, but by the time he proposed to her at the skating rink, she was as fond of him as she was of cashmere. She'd tried to figure out the precise time Roy stopped caring; she had it pinned somewhere between their first anniversary and the second time Maggie had said, "I'm really not in the mood, Roy."

Earning a living, paying the bills, and moving the trash containers to the road the night before collection day were responsibilities Roy met with aplomb. Being a supportive partner was where he fell short. It seemed to Maggie that an impenetrable wall had been built around him. Even when Allison Husk had hung herself in the capacious closet of her father's wood-paneled den, Roy expressed little sympathy and discouraged Maggie from flying to Savannah for the funeral. "It's not like you can relive old times," he'd muttered.

Roy cautiously navigated the eight miles home from his office through a veritable monsoon. Fierce winds whipped the elm trees, thick raindrops hammered the sunroof of Roy's Honda hatchback, and the windshield wipers struggled to clear the onslaught of water. He had never been happier to pull into the driveway, despite it being drenched with leaves. After hurrying into the house, Roy was taken aback by the lack of noise and activity. He half-expected his wife to greet him with a warm hug and a cold drink, chirping, "Dinner's almost ready." And he would smell the chicken and garlic and other scents wafting from the kitchen. But there were no comforting aromas of home cooking, no exuberant welcomes. His eyes darted around for signs of his wife: TV playing? No. Newspaper spread out on the coffee table? No. The place was eerily quiet and, because of the dim floor lamp illuminating the entire living room, the house took on a decidedly tomblike feel.

"Maggie?" he shouted. Silence. He stomped toward the kitchen. "Maggie?" Nothing. Not a pot on the stove. "Maggie, where are you?" he yelled as he headed to the hallway. He heard a low, muffled sound, like a weak groan, that seemed to be coming from the laundry room. It sounded vaguely like a wounded animal. With a baffled, quizzical expression, he followed the odd sound, heart pounding, afraid of what he'd find. He stepped into the laundry room and discovered Maggie curled up, head down, shoulders hunched, inside the Maytag dryer. "What the hell are you doing in there?" he shouted as he threw open the glass-front door. "Were you locked inside?" he asked.

"No, I wasn't locked in. I wanted to see how clothing feels in here, that's all."

"Is that all?" he inquired with sarcasm. "Give me your hand." Maggie dangled her arm and Roy guided her from one world to another. Once on the tiled floor, Maggie took a few moments to adjust to the jarring light and sudden change in air pressure. Roy studied her with a combination of pity and annoyance. "Do you really think clothing can feel?" he asked.

"Of course not," Maggie snapped.

"Well you just said you wanted to see how it feels."

"I know it doesn't feel the way a human does," she explained. "You're getting leaves all over the floor, Roy. Give me your wet clothes. I'll wash them."

Over cold chicken that turned out dry and creamed corn that was too creamy, Roy broached the subject gently. "Have you considered the possibility that you might need help?"

"I've been doing our laundry for six years without any help

and I don't see why I would want it now," Maggie stated. "Do you have a complaint about your clothes?" Heavy rain lashed the arched windows.

"No," he said apologetically. It was rare for Maggie to register even a hint of anger or exasperation, and when she did, it rattled him. "My clothes are the cleanest in the office. Sometimes I get compliments."

"Thank you," she responded. "That's nice to hear."

"Do any of your friends sit in their dryers, too?" he asked as nonchalantly as possible.

"I've never asked them. Why are you asking *me*?"

"Because I want to know if it's something you plan to do on a regular basis. I thought maybe it's a new fad in the neighborhood."

"I didn't *plan* to do anything, Roy. It was a spur of the moment action. To answer your question, I do not plan to do it on a regular basis and it's not a new fad. I like to try things *once*, and since I've tried this, it's unlikely I'll do it again."

"You don't plan to see how food feels in the refrigerator, do you?"

"My relationship with food is not what it is with laundry," she said.

Roy nodded gratefully, reached for the bottle of ketchup and drowned his chicken in it.

Maggie was nowhere to be found when Roy came home from the office the Wednesday before Easter Sunday. He let out a sigh when he discovered the laundry room inhabited by denims spinning around in the dryer and no trace of Maggie in either machine. When he called her name, the massive mound of clothing in the corner of the room moved, like an ant colony, as Maggie dug her way partially out from under the warm, dry garments. "I must've fallen asleep," she murmured, her face beaming with the glow of a woman who had just awakened next to her beloved, a glow Roy had never seen.

"Under the clothes?"

"They're clean," Maggie said, savoring the warmth of a pair of fleece pajamas hanging off her head. "Thoroughly washed and dried."

"When are we eating dinner?" Roy asked, through gritted teeth.

"I didn't make dinner," she confessed. "Are you very hungry?"

"Starving," he said.

Over a spinach and artichoke pizza that took twice as long as usual to be delivered, Roy asked his wife why she was doing laundry every single day. Maggie smoothed the linen napkin in her lap as her heart thumped in her chest. "My hours were cut at the museum," she finally admitted, "So I decided to make a little money by doing laundry for some neighbors."

"You're taking in laundry." Roy shook his head. "For which neighbors?"

"Just the ones on our street."

"Could you give me a few names, please?" he asked in a tone that barely hid his fury.

Nervously, Maggie cleared her throat, fidgeted with her fork. "The Fletchers, the Foleys, Hollis Broussard, uh...Nunnally Goodall, Donna Jean Jarvis, Marc and Honey Scott, uh...Rich Gitterman, the Hansens, Sheryl Linder."

"I see," he said, still repressing his rage. "So now the entire neighborhood thinks I can't make a decent living – that we have to take in laundry."

"No, they don't think that at all."

"Don't these people have their own damn machines?" He took a large, forceful bite of his pizza.

"Some of them do," Maggie explained. "But many of them don't have time to do laundry."

A thick piece of dough lodged itself in Roy's throat like an obese Santa in a thin chimney. He tried to swallow it but couldn't, tried to spit it out but couldn't. Panicked, he frantically pointed to his neck as his face turned the red of emergencies.

Maggie froze. Couldn't move a muscle. She knew what she was supposed to do thanks to CPR class, but her body wouldn't let her. She merely stared at Roy with eyes wide and mouth open. Finally, Roy managed to cough. The dough flew from his mouth and hurtled through the air like a cannonball. Maggie rose from her chair and picked up the small ball of dough. Then she carefully positioned it next to Roy's beer bottle.

Gasping for breath, Roy reached for his glass of water. Took a sip. "Maggie," he sternly said as soon as he was able to speak, "I want to have you evaluated."

"Like a rare coin?" she asked.

"No, not like that." Exasperated, Roy decided to postpone this particular conversation. Maggie remained silent through the rest of the meal, wondering if Roy realized his wife hadn't planned to save him from a violent choking death, and if he wondered why not.

The following evening, as Roy cursed a ridiculously long traffic light on his way home from work, Maggie stood in the cluttered laundry room, folding an embroidered blouse. Instead of adding the garment to the pile of finished clothing, she rested her hands on the sectional cross-stitch. Stroking the raised fabric in a gentle, almost loving fashion, she lost herself in the rich texture. A comforting warmth filled her, registering in every cell of her body. Eyes closed, Maggie imagined miniaturizing herself so that the stitches were mountains and she was surrounded by them, lost in their beauty and breadth, swallowed by them.

That night, in the cramped confines of her laundry room, Maggie came to a profound realization: washing clothes was her art. Nothing gave her more satisfaction than eliminating dirt and transforming a load of filthy, foul-smelling laundry into a neatly folded display of fresh, clean clothing. She found the passion that was missing in her passionless marriage. Sniffing a hot bath towel straight from the dryer was like lying in a field of lilies. The strong, clean scent of bleach aroused her in inexplicable ways. Warm, clean clothing was more than a mere comfort to Maggie; it was security, nourishment, sensuality. It was beginning anew with a perfectly clean slate.

Roy blasted into the house dripping wet after another Seattle rainstorm. The front door banged shut. He immediately spotted a line of a half dozen laundry baskets, overflowing with soiled garments. "What the hell is this?" he bellowed.

"What?" Maggie asked, stepping into the hallway. "Roy Skillet, you're soaking wet. Give me your shirt and I'll throw it in the next load."

"What is all this?" Roy asked again, his eyes darting from the baskets on the floor to his wife's flustered face.

"It's laundry, of course. I'm a surrogate mother who's given birth to a soft, cuddly load of cottons. I hand the newborns over to its mother who wears them and cares for them until it's time to do the routine all over again. These children never leave me. They always come back in need of washing."

Roy glanced around the room. "Is there a hidden camera here?"

"No," she said. "Now give me that damp shirt, it's in desperate need of washing."

"Are you for real? Because if you're for real, Maggie, you are one warped, crazy woman and I've had about enough of you."

"Roy," Maggie hissed with frustration. "The shirt."

"You care more about this damn shirt than you do about me."

"Don't be silly. Just take it off and hand it to me," she insisted.

"Listen carefully, Maggie, because I'm not going to whitewash this." Seething with anger, Roy focused on one full laundry basket after the next as if inspecting an enemy line-up. Maggie swept the closest basket into her arms as if protecting a small child. "It's either me or the laundry," he threatened.

"An ultimatum?" Maggie asked, squeezing the laundry basket. "Please don't make me choose. I hate ultimatums."

"I can't fucking believe I'm competing with dirty pants and filthy shirts. Choose right now," Roy insisted, realizing that his wife shared a level of intimacy with grimy clothing that she never shared with *him*.

Distressing as the ultimatum should have been and would have been before her awakening, Maggie stood unfazed. Roy stared at her, waiting. The whoosh of the dryer reminded Maggie that Nadine Verga's knits were revolving and needed to be removed soon, while Walter Blakely's whites were swirling in the washer. "I'm sorry Roy, I need a minute to check on something."

Roy didn't give his wife a minute. His left arm flew toward her face like a swinging baseball bat. She didn't wince; there wasn't time. The basket in Maggie's arms fell to the floor, and her body fell into the basket of Donna Jean Jarvis's denim skirts. Startled by his own actions, Roy stood his ground, heaving, trying to make sense of what happened. Suddenly fearful that Maggie might call the police, Roy raced to the front door, flung it open, and zoomed into rain that had relaxed into a whispering drizzle.

Shell shocked, Maggie didn't budge. Roy's open hand had slammed a tooth, and blood dripped from her mouth onto one of Donna Jean's skirts. Maggie decided not to call the police because she knew the damage was minor: a little hydrogen peroxide, a rinse in cold water, and the skirt would be good as new.

Word of Maggie's moonlighting gradually spread throughout town, and before long she was inundated with business. Some neighbors dropped their overflowing baskets off on their way to work. Some stopped by at noon. Pick-up time was from six o'clock to eight-thirty every evening. With the profits from her burgeoning business, Maggie purchased three new front load washers and two additional dryers. She began buying laundry detergent in bulk.

Roy was reaching his breaking point. Living with this woman and her loads of dirty clothing was damaging his self-esteem as well as his reputation. When some guy in the neighborhood tossed him a stained T-shirt and told him to give it to Maggie, he'd had enough.

He moved into a bland, one-bedroom place in a stucco maze of apartment dwellings. His new residence lacked direct sunlight and air-conditioning, as well as laundry facilities. Within two weeks, Roy was stepping over dirty clothes, packets of ketchup, matchbooks from the local strip club, and the occasional French fry. Dust accumulated on the furniture like light snow on a city street. Six-packs of beer took up most of his refrigerator. The only nutritious item in his cupboard was a can of albacore tuna left by a previous tenant.

One Sunday evening as the sun was setting, Maggie's doorbell rang. She found Roy on the welcome mat, clutching a large basket bulging with dirty clothes. Black bristles covered his neck and chin; he obviously hadn't shaved in days. "Hello, Maggie," he sighed. His heavy-lidded eyes were sad and vulnerable.

"Roy Skillet, do you need me to do your laundry?"

"I do." Though he said no more than the same two words he uttered on his wedding day, it was obvious he wanted more from Maggie than her professional services. As Maggie measured the proper amount of detergent, Roy stood in the doorway of the laundry room, watching her with keen interest. "You know exactly how much to pour in."

"It's not difficult," she responded matter-of-factly. "Is everything going well at work?"

"Not really," he said. "To tell you the truth, I might need to look for another job. Even though there's nothing I hate more than job hunting." It was obvious Roy had left his ego at home, or maybe had lost it entirely.

"I don't think anyone likes job hunting, Roy," Maggie told him.

Roy nodded. "Look at *you*! You started your own business. You didn't wait for someone to hire you."

"Are you saying you're proud of me?" she asked.

"Yes, I happen to be proud of you," he awkwardly admitted. This was a side of Roy Maggie had only seen once – when his younger sister survived an attack by a female grizzly bear and fought for her life in a hospital bed. Roy had been overloaded enough to break through his brick wall then. Now, in the doorway of the laundry room, the mortar holding the bricks together was crumbling again.

"It makes me happy that you're proud of me," she said.

"I'm not sure I even deserve your forgiveness," he said. "I've acted like a jackass."

"I didn't say I forgive you," Maggie replied coolly. "I just said I'm glad you're proud of me."

"Right," he responded, staring at the floor like a scolded child.

Maggie led Roy to the kitchen where they sipped decaf and nibbled on cherry pie as the laundry progressed through its cycles. It was Roy who got up to pour more coffee. It was Roy who washed the dishes after they finished their pie. Maggie sensed a distinct change in the air, as if a cool wind had begun blowing in her direction.

Later, when the dryer buzzed, they removed his clothes. Roy

searched for socks to make perfect pairs. Maggie folded her husband's crewneck T-shirts and chino shorts. The familiarity of this load brought Maggie a deep sense of comfort. She knew these clothes intimately and recalled each separate item with fondness. She even discovered the rich texture of Roy's plum-colored poplin polo that she'd never noticed before. Maybe, she thought, a few surprises might still await her.

The clearing of Roy's throat alerted Maggie that a topic rich with importance was about to be broached. Maggie put Roy's blue pajama bottoms down to give him her complete attention. "Could you teach me the right way to fold a long-sleeve shirt?" he asked, wrapping his arm around her waist.

Liquor Store Lust

WITH HER SILKY BLACK HAIR, almond eyes, and legs that seemed to reach Mexico City, Suzy Herzog of Aurora, Illinois had turned heads since she was twelve. Every single day, at least one person told her she was gorgeous enough to become a model, but Suzy's heart was set on beveled-glass design.

When Suzy turned eighteen, though, she held up a liquor store and changed the course of her life.

The liquor store heist was executed out of desperation, and like most teenage decisions, it seemed like a smart idea at the time. Suzy needed a substantial sum of money to pay for the tonsillectomy of her nine-year-old sister, Nadine. The stalwart school nurse insisted the enlarged tonsils be removed immediately, but Suzy was too proud to confess that her dirt-poor parents could barely pay the rent, let alone cough up the cash for an in-patient medical procedure.

Before resorting to robbery, Suzy considered a dozen scenarios. She applied for a bank loan, but the request was denied by the hard-boiled branch manager. She implored her neighbor Zelda to lend her the money, but the adventurous octogenarian was saving for a trip to Reno. She pleaded with her Aunt Gert and Uncle Otto for financial help, but Otto's hours at the slaughterhouse had been slashed, and Gert was unemployed due to a hip injury from a Ferris wheel fall.

Tonsils, or the removal of them, did not rank high on the priority list of Ryoko and Rolf Herzog, both of whom trudged through their lives and their graveyard shifts at the gas station in a cloud of marijuana-induced haze. Usually high or inebriated when their daughters got home from school, they shirked their parental responsibilities to such a startling extent that food was often sacrificed for booze and pot. Before she was old enough to understand, Suzy noticed the eleven-ounce tumbler in Ryoko's hand from noon until night, and she wondered why her mother was always thirsty.

Suzy often slept over at her best friend Jeannette's house. One Sunday morning, she tiptoed to the Midgen den and rifled through the wooden desk in search of a pair of scissors to cut off a pesky curl that hung annoyingly over her forehead. When she came across a sleek little pistol, she froze. Struck by a bolt of inspiration, Suzy seized the weapon. It felt surprisingly comfortable in her hands. She knew exactly what she had to do.

Just before midnight on Christmas Eve, she climbed into her father's beat-up Volkswagen Rabbit. Clutching the steering wheel with sweaty palms, the eighteen-year-old beauty roared down the dark, deserted road. The wind whistled like a tea kettle, but the air was unseasonably, unreasonably warm: June weather in December.

In the deserted parking lot, Suzy was relieved to see that the burger joint and beauty salon were closed. Still, she felt like a giant raw nerve. With trepidation, she stumbled out of the car and headed toward the liquor store.

Suzy hadn't expected the guy behind the counter: industrial-strength smile, dark blond hair tumbling toward his shoulders, large tat on a muscled bicep. Name tag read Troy. "Hey," he said with a sexy grin. "Can I help you find something?"

Suzy felt a river of warmth flow through her, like a sugar rush only not as jittery. "Are we alone?" she asked, thinking some lonely soul might've been browsing the booze.

"Totally," he smiled. "Just you and me." The sexual electricity was palpable.

Suzy's heart raced. A novice in the art of burglary, she wasn't sure what to do next. A manual for this didn't exist. "Uh, could you lock the front door please?" she asked.

Troy dashed over to the glass entrance, and Suzy was riveted by his smooth, agile motion: a cheetah silently charging through the jungle. "Done," he proudly announced after bolting the door from the bottom. "What else can I do to make you feel comfortable?" he asked, his eyes scanning her body.

"Take me behind the counter," she said. A surge of excitement bubbled inside her.

He gently took Suzy's hand and led her to the alcove surrounded by candy bars and bottles of booze. The moment he let go, Suzy pulled out the pistol from the front pocket of her shorts. "Take the money from the cash register and load it into a bag, please," she requested.

Troy thought this was a joke, that the gun was probably a water pistol. "What are my options?" He played along, grinning.

"Well," she said, "I guess you do what I say or breathe your last breath." Suzy could hardly believe she was speaking these horrifying words.

"That's like Hobson's choice, huh?"

"Is he the day manager?" Suzy asked.

"No, that's Hansen."

"Take the money from the cash register and load it into a bag," she repeated.

Knowing he could overpower her if necessary, he went along with the scheme and grabbed a large brown bag from below the counter. Then he opened the register and removed the bills. "Done," he announced.

"Throw in a couple of peanut butter cups," she instructed.

"Done." Troy paused. "Why are you doing this?"

"Because my sister needs her tonsils taken out," she explained. "Now take off that T-shirt and those jeans. Kneel on the floor."

Troy stripped in five seconds flat. The sight of his nude body, even more ripped than the jeans, gave Suzy a rush; she wanted to touch every part of him. She peeled off her clothing, and before she knew it, he was on top of her, moving and grinding. Her free hand ran down the back of his sinewy body. "Please put a condom on."

"I don't have one," he sighed, tracing a finger down her stomach.

"They're right over there," she said, using the pistol to point to the colorful display.

"Oh, right." He bolted up, ripped one open, and put it on.

Suzy had already lost her virginity to Jonathan Shevlove, the lanky veterinarian, but that initial experience, amid the sound of ailing, barking dogs, wasn't terribly terrific or even mildly memorable. She wanted to try it again with Troy, whose rippling arms and tight butt were the quintessence of female desire.

As he entered her, all five of Suzy's senses crackled at full capacity. She touched, she bit, she watched his butt bob up and down. She listened to his gasps and her own, and she smelled his subtle body odor. His flowing hair covered Suzy's head like a curtain, and his primal passion took her to heights she didn't know existed. When she thought she reached the pinnacle, Troy took her higher still, sending her soaring through the stratosphere. "Don't stop," she screeched, wrapping her shaking legs around him.

"Not going to," he groaned as his excitement built. But the end came all too soon. "Done," he whispered into her ear, head resting between her shoulder and the side of her neck.

"Now tell me you love me," she dizzily instructed.

"Huh? I hardly know you," he gasped.

Suzy reached for the gun that she had safely tucked under the bag of cash, and she shoved it into his bare back. "I love you," he yelped, recoiling from the gun by pressing harder against her. "You're the girl for me. My one and only."

"I love you too," she replied tenderly, lightly kissing his eyelids and running her hands through his thick mane of hair. Troy was becoming aroused again. Suzy was ready for another go. A soft kiss became deep in a matter of seconds, and their passion was tamed only by the arrival of red and blue flashing lights that brightened the dark from the other side of the glass.

"Come out with your hands above your head," a disembodied male voice boomed through a megaphone.

"Oh my God," Suzy cried.

Unbeknownst to the young lovers, six squad cars had silently swarmed into the parking lot as a result of the liquor store's surveillance camera and its link to the local police station.

The teenagers threw on their clothing in the moving light. Troy, his nerves noticeably jangled, quivered as he zipped his pants. He prayed that the police wouldn't search the locked drawer behind the counter and find his stash of pot. Suzy was brimming with so many emotions she could hardly distinguish one from another.

Before she knew it, Suzy was in handcuffs, being led out of the store by a burly officer. The parking lot, teeming with uniformed men, looked like a police convention, but Suzy appeared preternaturally calm. In fact, upon close inspection she seemed positively aglow. Troy had tapped into a part of her she didn't know existed. For the first time in her young life, she knew what it felt like to be hopelessly in love – it felt like discovering the moon.

Troy didn't want to press charges, but his outraged parents insisted. A media circus ensued, bringing enormous, unwanted attention to the Herzog family. The story made local headlines. News vans were parked on the lawn. Every member of the Herzog family became fair game. Nadine was taken away from Ryoko and Rolf by a no-nonsense representative of Child Welfare Services. Her tonsillectomy was performed without a hitch (paid for by the state), and she was placed in a foster home with two caring parents, three older sisters and a baby guinea pig.

Suzy was carted off to a high-security correctional facility for women.

Prison was no picnic: three supervised showers a week. No mirrors in the cells. No catalogue shopping or internet use. But a friendship with fellow inmate Cherry Charbonneau, a post-op, made life tolerable.

During her first six weeks as a caged criminal, Suzy could barely stop gushing about Troy, recounting her tale of robbery and desire to Cherry, Jo-Jo, Elna, Two-By-Four, and the other incarcerated gals. When she spoke, she saw his face, felt his touch, relived the rapture. In her deranged longing, she came alive. Then one day, not only did Suzy stop mentioning him, her effervescent personality vanished. During woodwork shop, Cherry pulled her aside. "What wrong, baby?" she asked. "You not your usual bubbly self."

"Now it hurts just to think about him," she admitted. "I miss him so much I can hardly stand it."

"Well, you be out of this hell hole soon."

"You think he'd want to date a girl who held him up?" she asked.

"You make a mistake, that's all. Besides, he told you he loves you."

"Yeah, with a gun in his back."

Some nights, lying in her dreary shoebox of a cell, Suzy thought she might lose what was left of her mind. Repressing urges to pull the hair from her head or bite her flesh till it bled, she shut her heavy-lidded eyes and clutched the ragged mattress, hands in throbbing fists. She'd known loneliness before, but this was a different sort; this was suffocating.

During Suzy's fourth month behind bars, the anguish began to fade. With the passing of each identical week, she began thinking less and less of Troy because she began thinking less and less about *anything*. Picking herself up each morning and trudging through her daily activities, Suzy had become a robotic version of her previous self, immune to gray walls, prison grub, and prison garb.

Suzy reacted without emotion when she heard that her childhood house had burned to the ground, her parents still in it. Ryoko and Rolf had been drinking and smoking when they passed out. A lit cigarette set a paper bag on fire, and it wasn't long before the walls, roof, and furniture were engulfed in flames, turning everything, including the flesh and bones of her parents, into ash.

Toward the end of Suzy's seven-month sentence (reduced from eleven for good behavior), she was living in a fog, not unlike her now-deceased parents, and had almost forgotten about Troy. Following a tearful farewell with her fellow inmates, Suzy withdrew the paltry amount of money that had been sitting in her bank account and headed south, through Kentucky, Tennessee, and Georgia, straight into Florida.

South Beach was a town Suzy had always wanted to visit; she saw it as a magical destination, a haven, like the Land of Oz. But she was immediately intimidated by the city and its populace. Her ratty outfits were conspicuous next to everyone's cutting-edge style, and her alabaster skin literally paled in comparison to the native deep golden tans.

Perched on a bench on a leafy street in Little Havana, she sipped from a tall Starbucks cup. A middle-aged guy in a gray Gucci T-shirt plopped down next to her. She thought he had the face of a salamander. "You could be a real looker," he said, "but you need to buy new clothes, get some color, and do something with your mop of hair."

"I'll work on it as soon as I finish my coffee," she replied coldly.

"You have potential. I know potential when I see it." Confidence oozed from this amphibian like oil from a gushing well.

"Thanks for the vote of confidence. That and $3.50 will buy me another latte."

"I like your sense of humor," he persisted.

Suzy looked the guy straight in the eye. "Why don't you cut through the bullcrap and tell me what you want."

"I want to know what you do for a living."

"I hold up liquor stores," she nonchalantly replied.

He laughed. "My name is Marky McGinnis." He reached into the pocket of his dark jeans, removed a leather business card holder, and handed Suzy a card. "I run a modeling agency. If you clean yourself up, you could have a career, make ten grand a day. Work in New York, Paris, Milan. Become a sought-after face, a catwalk queen, a calendar girl. But don't call me until you make yourself over, and I'm talking head-to-toe."

"I'll think about nothing else," she sighed.

Marky McGinnis rose from the bench and strolled away, his Kenneth Cole Oxfords clacking on the sidewalk. Suzy shook her head as she hauled herself down the street to a liquor store.

As she entered, Suzy flashed back to that fateful night. A warm rush flowed through her body until she saw the clerk behind the counter. He was certainly no Troy.

She bought a tuna sandwich, a bottle of Ketel One and a container of orange juice. Up her sleeve was a candy bar she shoplifted, and inside her flip-flop was a small packet of peanuts she'd retrieved from the floor with her toes. Feeling a deep sleep coming on, Suzy checked into a creaky old art deco motel a half-mile from the ocean.

She sat unsteadily on the dingy double bed in dim light, downing one drink after another. The low rumbling of the ice machine on the other side of the wall sounded like a weapon of mass destruction firing up. The sound unnerved her and compelled her to keep drinking.

Suzy caught sight of Marky McGinnis's business card that she'd left on the circular side table. She picked it up and stared. "A calendar girl," she muttered with a chuckle. Then she lit a match and brought the flame to the rectangular card. It burst into bright orange heat. The combination of vodka and noxious smoke made Suzy pass out and drop the card on the bed. Within five minutes, a huge fire roared.

Thick gray smoke engulfed the room, and Suzy coughed into consciousness. The heat from the fire was terrifying, and she leapt out of bed like an Olympic gymnast. She managed to jump from her two-story window, breaking an arm and a rib in the process. Suzy was relieved to be alive, grateful to have avoided a death similar to that of her parents.

Within ten minutes, sirens were blasting and fire engines crowded the street, but the linens, mattresses, carpet, drapes, phone books, and phones in the motel had already turned to ash – not to mention the pillows, towels, toilet paper, lamp shades, lamps, and tiny bottles of shampoo.

Suzy backed away from the noise and the commotion, trying her best to appear inconspicuous. She decided to clean herself up head to toe, as the salamander suggested. Then she would make a few bucks. Then she would search for her sister Nadine, and hope that a guy with a large tat on his bicep was searching for *her*.

Aromatherapy

NEWS OF THE MURDER spread rapidly through the sleepy suburb of Seven Springs, Minnesota, a quaint little town that seemed untouched by the 21st century. There'd never been a murder in Seven Springs; there'd never even been much news. But here it was. Sixty-year-old mustard heiress Marie Poupon-Kennedy had stopped breathing in Room B of the Seven Springs Serenity Spa during a Gentle Oxygenating Facial. Phuong Pruitt, the considerate Vietnamese clinician, had applied an exfoliating almond-honey mask to her client's face, along with a cucumber eye compress. She'd then stepped out to allow the products to work their magic while Marie relaxed to Mahler's *Symphony Number 6*.

Phuong took a few sips of citrus-enhanced water and grabbed a bunch of the grapes nested in ceramic bowls throughout the hallways. She headed to the back yard and sat quietly on the wooden bench facing the aromatic rose garden, thinking about the petty argument she had with her stubborn sister. Two minutes of fresh air later, she returned to remove Marie's mask.

Estheticians were accustomed to the occasional client nodding off in the thickly-cushioned reclining chair, so Phoung thought nothing of Marie Poupon-Kennedy's head leaning dramatically to the left. Upon closer inspection, however, she noticed that the neck glowed with a bright scarlet abrasion. The heiress had been strangled.

Phuong's scream was so blood-curdling that it ejected nude and semi-nude clients from their detox mud baths and salt glow body scrubs. Yvette, the veteran masseuse, raced to Phuong and pulled her into the hallway, as far from the corpse as possible. In a few shocking seconds, the serenity of the Seven Springs Serenity Spa was replaced with pandemonium.

With breasts bouncing and bracelets jiggling, Irma Schifflet, the strawberry blonde owner of the day spa, came scurrying down the hallway. "Quiet down, everyone!" she shouted, her voice sputtering like a car on its last drop of gasoline. "Yvette, would you call the paramedics please? And then the police." Yvette hurried down the hall. "Everything is under control," Irma assured her terrified staff. Though she knew precisely what to say and how to say it, she felt like she was disintegrating, as if her organs were falling from their designated spots.

Five minutes later, six Seven Springs police officers were inspecting the spa, now designated a crime scene. "Can we talk in private?" Officer Hugh Capers asked Irma conspiratorially, hands jammed in his pockets. Irma maneuvered her right arm through his left, and led him into her cozy office, redolent of lilac.

Desperately trying to disguise her state of quasi-hysteria, Irma looked the officer straight in the eye. "Before you ask a single question," she stated, "you need to understand something. It's quite common for an esthetician to leave the room for several minutes at a time." She conveyed this information with confident authority that belied her ultra-feminine aura.

"We haven't accused anybody of anything," Capers said.

"Of course you haven't, you just arrived. But chances are you'll want to pin this on someone, and I'll tell you right now: Phuong Pruitt didn't do it."

"I'll keep that in mind," he responded.

"Please do."

"Smells good in here," Capers remarked.

"I'm glad you think so," Irma said, pointing to a colorful display. "Those are our essential oils: lavender, jasmine, sweet pea, rose. It's been proven that fragrance enters the brain and impacts our mood. You should try one of our aromatherapy sessions sometime. On the house."

"Thanks, I'll consider it," he said, leaning forward. Irma saw hunger in his eyes, and knew he was mentally undressing her from her bangle bracelets and low-cut top. She caught his eye and he instantly looked away. "What's that wrench doing next to that fragrance?" he asked.

Panicked, Irma darted over to the display, wondering if the metal tool might be construed as a murder weapon. "A plumber was here yesterday to fix a leak. He must've left it by accident," she grabbed the wrench and hid it behind a stack of books.

"Would you mind telling me the name of the plumber?"

"Of course not," she hesitated. "We use Randal Beuden, The Drain Surgeon."

Capers wrote the name down on a small pad of paper. The gaze he fixed on her next was as sexually intense as anything she'd felt in many months. "Choker, huh?" he asked.

"I beg your pardon?" Irma asked, so flustered she held her breath.

"The choker you're wearing. It's pretty."

"Oh yes," she sighed with relief. "It's rhinestone."

"Looks good on you. But almost anything would look good on you." The officer sheepishly grinned.

Suddenly Irma's delicate body erupted in the loudest, most

intense sneeze of its existence. Thoroughly embarrassed, she reached for a scented tissue and dabbed her nose. "Accuse me," she mumbled.

"What did you say?" Capers asked.

"Excuse me."

"Oh. Of course. Gesundheit. How well did you know Marie Poupon-Kennedy?" he asked, abruptly getting back to business.

"About as well as anyone in this town," she said.

"Did she have any enemies?"

"To be honest, Marie had a lot of enemies. She would stab you in the back, then sashay off to lunch without a care in the world. But she was a client, so we treated her with respect, just as we treat all our clients."

"I'm sure you did."

Irma's phone buzzed, shattering the calm so fiercely that she convulsed and fell off her chair. Capers instantly rushed to help. "Are you all right?" he inquired.

"Yes, thank you so much," she whispered, gazing into his dark eyes and holding onto his warm hand. He helped her find her way back into the desk chair. She reached for the receiver with a quivering arm, as if sitting on a vibrating platform. "Yes? I see. How many? Thank you, Ingrid." She hung up. "The media," she said to Capers. "They've invaded like a SWAT team. Seven Springs Star-Ledger, Daily Kenoshan, WGAG-TV, WDOA. They're all here."

The frenzy wasn't unexpected; the victim was a local celebrity. Marie Poupon-Kennedy had recently acquired several stores in the downtown district of Seven Springs including Uncle Bert's Hardware, Dimbleby's Gourmet Cheese, The Drain Surgeon, Francine's Fried Chicken, and the International Children's Dance Academy. But the purchase that raised the most eyebrows was City Hall. The six million dollar transaction confirmed everyone's worst fear: Marie Poupon-Kennedy was single-handedly taking over the town. It was rumored that the mustard heiress was interested in buying the Seven Springs Serenity Spa and re-naming it the Marie Poupon-Kennedy Serenity Center.

The old woman's actions enraged the small business owners of Seven Springs who had worked tirelessly to transform the grimy downtown area into the gorgeous, thriving oasis it finally became. They weren't going to let some super-wealthy bitch march in and buy their land, tear down their shops and boutiques, and intimidate good people into selling their property.

Marie Poupon-Kennedy wasn't strangled by one pair of hands; there were thirty sets around that long, wrinkled neck. If one person was arrested, all thirty would be nabbed. That was the decision made one week before the mustard heiress arrived for her fatal facial, and the words of Randal Beuden reverberated in Irma's head: "Sometimes extreme measures need to be taken."

"Absolutely," Arlene Tibbles added. "To maintain our very lives and livelihoods. You'll be a hero, Irma. For the rest of your life you'll be the quiet, unsung hero who saved our community."

At the moment, sitting across from Officer Capers, Irma didn't feel the least bit heroic. Consumed with fear, she struggled to hold it together. "I'm a bit freaked out," she confessed. "Nobody ever died in the day spa before."

"It had to happen eventually."

"Really?" she asked. Capers nodded, and Irma wondered if he did so just to make her feel better. "Everyone outside will want to talk to us," she told him.

"I'm sure they will, but first I should check with my guys to see if they located a murder weapon," Capers declared.

Like iron drawn to a magnet, Irma's hand descended to her crotch which hid the thin cord that had been wrapped around Poupon-Kennedy's neck. "Yes, of course," she nervously muttered. "A murder weapon would tell you a lot."

"It's the first step toward apprehending the killer."

"The first step, yes. Then perhaps we could talk to the media together."

"Excellent idea," he replied, gazing into Irma's soft green eyes. "We'll do it together." He'd already decided that he would ask her out for a steak and shrimp dinner on Saturday night.

Saturday morning had given birth to dark skies, heavy winds and a ghoulish apparition on the front lawn of Irma's small, one-story brick house. Irma saw everything clearly and felt the frail female spirit profoundly. She even detected the faint scent of Dijon-style mustard. By late afternoon, the winds had died down and the threat of a major storm seemed distant, but an eerie blue-gray mist hovered.

In a thick fog, Irma poured herself a glass of grape juice mixed with Merlot. She sleepwalked into the living room and looked around, as if seeing it for the first, or last, time. Sinking into the overstuffed white cushions on the sofa, she accidentally spilled some of her drink, but she was too comatose to notice. Like ink spilling onto damp paper, the purple stain spread several inches until it resembled a human heart. She closed her eyes and basked in the comfort of the cushions.

The combination of fresh orange zinnias and pink Peruvian lilies sweetened the air but couldn't disguise the sour smell that had arrived with the mist. Irma reached for two small containers on the coffee table. The label on the tranquilizer read: "Take two tablets by mouth as needed for anxiety." She poured out a couple of pills, tossed them on her tongue, and forced them down her throat with a gulp of her juice and wine. The label for the sleeping aid read: "Take one tablet orally as needed for insomnia." She shoved two in her mouth.

Flipping the channels of her flat-screen TV, she bypassed a lame game show, a Ben Stiller movie, CNN, women's college volleyball, and a Cameron Diaz comedy. A black and white documentary on Discovery caught her attention. An elephant was tearing through tropical Africa, and Irma had always been fascinated with wild animals. Going on a safari had been a pipe dream. The majestic mammal ran for its life, as a deep-voiced narrator spoke. "Because of the value of their ivory, especially in the Chinese market, poaching in Kenya is on the rise." Irma poured three small white beads into her hand, and swallowed them with a hearty sip, trying to dissolve the guilt that had begun to settle in. She wondered if the poachers felt even a morsel of guilt.

More than 100,000 elephants had been killed in Kenya over a twenty-year period, the narrator explained. Without taking her eyes off the screen, Irma grabbed the sleeping aids, counted six tablets, and tossed them in her mouth. Another swig of her drink washed them down her throat. She picked up the tranquilizer container and turned it to its side, allowed a half dozen to fall into her palm. She licked her hand until the tiny white dots were stuck to her tongue. Then, with another sip, she smiled lazily to herself. A fusillade of bullets emerged from the guns of a small army of poachers. The boom forced Irma's body to jerk, as if bombarded with a bolt of electricity. Once the defenseless animal lay lifeless on the ground, Irma tasted the salt of her tears that she hadn't realized were on her face. "Annihilation," she muttered.

She washed the last ten pills down her throat with one large swig. In a haze of hopelessness, she lifted her legs and stretched out, realizing that certain actions offered no second chances. Gazing at the screen, she listened to the commanding voice of the narrator: "The elephant is a particularly intelligent creature. When wandering through a camp in which poaching has taken place, it ignores the bones of every slaughtered animal until it comes upon those of the elephant. With its trunk, the live animal inspects the remains. The elephant knows the massacre that's been performed on one of its own."

"Oh my God," Irma whispered, shutting her wet, weary eyes, shielding herself from the horror. She fell back onto the soft white pillow that shifted to accommodate her, as if making a mold of her head.

Two hours later, Officer Hugh Capers, freshly showered and shaved, teeth brushed and flossed until his gums bled, rang Irma's doorbell. Precisely on time to pick her up for their date, the officer waited on Irma's weatherworn welcome mat in his blue blazer and new hush puppies, enjoying the scent of the dozen pink roses in his arms.

When Irma didn't come to the door after twenty seconds, he rang the bell again.

The Father of Dental Floss

(This story contains 5% fact.)

EACH YEAR, OVER THREE MILLION MILES OF DENTAL FLOSS are sold in the U.S. alone. A recent survey conducted by the *Journal of Oral Rehabilitation* and *InStyle Magazine* concluded that 48% of Americans feel guilty because they don't floss on a regular basis, and 97% feel even guiltier for lying to their dentists about it. If they knew the colorful history of dental floss, these people might treat flossing like a sacred ritual as opposed to a nagging chore.

It was a time of grandeur and greed, astonishing wealth and staggering poverty. It was a place where pomp and ceremony flourished next to pimps and sacrilege: New Orleans, 1815, with its heavy drinking, heavy partying, and heavy petting between slave owners and nubile slave girls.

Pubs. Clubs. Poorly lit slave quarters late at night. Inebriated men and women, cavorting to their hearts' content, oblivious to the germs they harbored in their rancid Dixie mouths. With gingivitis, periodontitis, plaque, tooth rot, and severely infected gums, the people of New Orleans were (unbeknownst to them) being orally poisoned.

One man took notice.

He may have entered the world a Yankee (in Braintree, Vermont) but Levi Parmly found success below the Mason-Dixon Line. For decades, gums and teeth were this family's bread and butter. Hailing from a long line of dental professionals, he kept the legacy alive.

Levi was a visionary, the very first dentist to insist his patients clean their teeth with a piece of silk string called floss. This procedure seemed preposterous to a lot of people. In the early 1800s, it was highly unpopular to put anything but food and a toothbrush in one's mouth, and to a few priggish members of the upper crust, Parmly was a periodontal pariah.

Dental floss didn't become available to the consumer until after Levi's death in 1859, when the first patent for floss was awarded to Johnson & Johnson in 1898. He didn't live to see his creation embraced by American mouths, but his heirs are fighting tooth and nail (no pun intended) to keep the name of their ancestor alive.

Carly and Pearl Parmly of Poplar Bluff, Missouri are the great, great, great, great, great granddaughters of the great dentist. Half-sisters, they had the same father but vastly different mothers. One was a *chanteuse* of French extraction, the other a forklift operator of Brazilian heritage. The proudest achievement of the half-siblings is the unique tooth museum they created in honor of Levi. Nestled in the foothills of the Ozark Mountains, a stone's throw from Lake Wappapello, stands The Parmly Open-Air Museum of Tooth Care & Floss Vigilance. This one-of-a-kind archive fills the den and spills into the lush, two thousand square foot back yard of the Parmly estate. Visitors from every part of the globe are treated to fascinating displays of mouth mirrors, dental bridges, crown removers, drills, syringes and tongue holding forceps.

Not only does Carly boast chalk-white teeth and glowing gums, she stands with impeccable posture. In fact, she can balance a hardcover copy of *A Proper Guide to the Management of the Teeth* (Levi's pioneering book of 1819) on her head while rinsing. All blondness, breasts and teeth, she dresses in traditional Hawaiian muumuus, flowing and loose fitting, without undergarments. Always barefoot, she occasionally purrs like a cat for no discernible reason. Some say that if her skin were to be cut, it would bleed honey.

If Carly is the self-proclaimed boss of the floss, Pearl is the wisdom tooth of the operation. She's the quiet half-sister, but her reticence belies her passionate conviction. Dressed like one about to embark on a white-water expedition, the no-nonsense Parmly carefully checks the mouths of all museum visitors as they exit, making sure each tooth has been flossed to perfection at one of the available sinks. Pearl has been called everything from the Tooth Nazi to a modern-day Stalin with string. "I'm here to clean teeth, not to make lunch buddies," she barks. "Food particles are partial to our gums the way bees are partial to honey, so it's essential to floss after every meal, whether you devoured a chicken fried steak, southern fried chicken, an ear of lettuce or a head of corn."

The museum casts a spell so powerful that more than a few guests are compelled to drop everything and brush their teeth right then and there, and Carly made it possible for them to do just that. Dotting the grounds are a dozen white pedestal sinks attached to small walnut tables packed with tools of the trade. Toothbrushes are available for purchase at the concession stand. Toothpaste and floss are on the house. It's not uncommon to see visitors frantically flossing as those around them leisurely stroll, many with teething babies in their arms.

Every inch of the place is impressive, and Carly is terribly proud, but she won't sleep easily – in the luxurious canopy bed she shares with Pearl – until the public becomes aware of her great, great, great, great, great grandfather's contribution to science and fresh breath. "He was a true pioneer who truly possessed a keen perspicacity about dentistry that few ever had, not to mention the sheer percipience of the importance of oral hygiene to the body's overall health," Carly has stated publicly.

Her obsession began years ago when she convinced her pharmacist to give her a small percentage of the profit from every package of floss he sold. As part of the deal, she agreed to floss him in the pharmacy's back room every evening. Because the arrangement worked out so well, Carly cultivated similar relationships with pharmacists in neighboring towns. Thanks to fair enterprise, she became one of the ten wealthiest women in Missouri and decided to use the money to open this museum that quickly became a "must-see" for tourists visiting the state and tooth aficionados from near and far.

An expert in everything oral, Carly is a one-woman crusade to make flossing fun. That's why she created *flavored* floss. This tasty package is making the rounds of mouths from Seattle to Secaucus to South Beach with a variety of flavors to appeal to the hard-to-please kid as well as the fussy adult. There's apple, grape, watermelon, citrus, salami, pistachio, chocolate mousse, Chilean sea bass, whipped cream dream, French fry, beef stew, Jamaican screw, brandy, tuna and horseradish – a taste for every set of teeth.

Carly has a warning for those who refuse to floss: "Your future will consist of porcelain crowns, chronic pain, and root canals."

Recently, the Parmly half-sisters were stunned to hear about an extremist group determined to ban dental floss from the world market. "Take it off your shelves!" these radicals shout in unison while marching on public streets in front of pharmacies, supermarkets and tackle shops. This band of revolutionaries is convinced the product contains inherent danger as there have been a surprising number of floss-driven escape attempts from American prisons. A West Virginia convict traded cigarettes for floss and created a rope long enough to climb over the prison's eighteen-foot wall, only to be captured and sentenced to an additional five years in the slammer. In 1988, three convicts climbed out a window of New York's Metropolitan Correction Center and slid down six stories on a dental floss rope. They were caught, and part of their punishment was supervised flossing twice a day in front of a panel of fellow inmates.

The official spokesperson for these fervent anti-flossers is Mamie Flay-Sheehan of Des Moines, Iowa. "Every time I see a package of dental floss," the divorced mother of two says, "I imagine a burly, strapping escaped convict forcing my teenage daughter to strip to her skivvies and perform all the cheers she created as head cheerleader. Then he would demand a shoulder and neck massage, with her budding breasts pinned to his back."

Carly and Pearl don't take the Flay-Sheehan threat very seriously. They believe dental floss has become a staple of the American bathroom like liquid soap and shaving cream. Will intelligent people toss their floss away in a knee-jerk reaction to a few creative convicts? Carly doesn't think so. "Dental floss is like our postal service," she says as she relaxes on the front porch, away from all the noise and activity. "Nothing can stop it: not rain, sleet, snow or some paranoid dame from Des Moines."

The facts:.

- Levi Spear Parmly was a real person who lived in New Orleans and created dental floss.

- A Proper Guide to the Management of the Teeth was Levi's pioneering book of 1819.

- The first patent for floss was awarded to Johnson & Johnson in 1898, after Parmly's death.

- Incarcerated convicts really used dental floss in aborted attempts to escape from prison.

- There are no Parmly great great great great great grandchildren who created a tooth museum.

Ophelia's Fortieth

Laurel Finnegan loathed going to parties by herself, but all her friends seemed to be on some exotic trip to one of the thousand places they're supposed to see before they die. Unfortunately, this particular *soiree* was one Laurel didn't want to miss. With the support of one tiny tranquilizer, she decided to take the plunge and attend the party solo.

The event in question was Ophelia Gamble's fortieth birthday. Beautifully dressed straight people and even more beautifully dressed gay men stood on the hardwood floors of Ophelia's penthouse apartment, some clutching champagne flutes filled with Cristal, others holding crystal wine goblets brimming with pinot noir. Smoldering cigarettes dangled from busy lips, and Laurel seriously wondered how long the ubiquitous red roses would last in the ubiquitous white smoke.

Because of a preponderance of female size zero specimens, Laurel felt like a pork sausage at a convention of carrot sticks. Still, she tried to stand tall in her black suede heels and sleeveless black dress, and exude a sense of *joie de vivre*, no matter how anemic her *joie*.

A jovial bald man sat at the baby grand, knocking out show

tunes. Friendly servers in military jackets roamed from room to crowded room carrying trays of vegetarian appetizers. They didn't even *attempt* to get near the balcony, teeming with people gasping for fresh air on this unseasonably nippy July night.

Not long after Laurel's arrival, the hand of an emaciated woman, more bone than flesh, gripped Laurel's bare upper arm. The stranger's purple hair and burgundy dress happened to blend beautifully with Ophelia's lilac living room walls. "Sorry," she gasped, trying to catch her breath, find her balance and avoid falling on the floor.

"Are you all right?" Laurel asked.

"Never been worse," she replied as she let go of Laurel's arm and rushed into the crowd, the burgundy dress revealing her dramatically bony back. The experience left Laurel unnerved. She worried that something was severely wrong.

With cranberry juice-and-vodka in hand, she milled into a swirl of conversation snippets:

"It wasn't an asylum, sweetheart; it was a healthspa called The Asylum."

"Sex is like a vacation. You don't always want to goto the same place."

"He makes things happen, Lance. You just letthem happen."

"Why that quack hasn't been reported to theAcademy of Plastic Surgery is beyond me."

"The man brought dignity to everything he did,except when he plied that Girl Scout with gingimlets."

Laurel found a place to park herself near the piano player, who wowed the crowd with *June is Bustin' Out All Over. An odd piece to play in July*, she thought. A six-footer with the dapper look of a TV doctor stood a few feet away. His chin was strong and his dark hair rippled back in waves from his forehead. He politely nodded when their eyes met, then straightened his pants and posture.

Laurel realized the guy held her gaze a fraction of a second too long for him to be gay. His gradual steps toward her confirmed. "Hello," he greeted. "I'm Patrick."

A strand of hair was hanging on his sleeve, the only blemish on an otherwise immaculate outfit. Laurel delicately pulled it off. "Hi," she responded. "Laurel."

An expression of sublime satisfaction bloomed on Patrick's face, as if Laurel had just offered to be his sex slave and full-time cook and housekeeper.

Patrick asked Laurel how she knew Ophelia. "We were in the same class," she explained, studying him. "It was years after college, a night course in French Rococo and Neoclassic art. I want to *be* her when I grow up," Laurel confessed. There was always some African safari or Mediterranean cruise in the works for Ophelia, not to mention some jet-setting CEO, but she still found time to teach underprivileged children to read. In contrast, Laurel's life was a series of dull days at a midtown consulting firm and dreary nights in a downtown apartment with no future plans except for babysitting her two nephews in Brooklyn. "Just look at the extravaganza she throws for a simple birthday."

"I might hire her for my next one."

"Book in advance," Laurel advised. "She's in demand."

"Excellent idea."

She liked this man. Despite the polished appearance, there was a kind of sweet simplicity to him. She couldn't help noticing the attentive way he listened, and she wondered why such a great guy was alone on a Saturday night. Curiosity was compelling her to ask, but she had the good sense to restrain herself.

"How do *you* know Ophelia?" she asked.

Just as Patrick was about to respond, a blood-curdling scream came careening from the balcony, shredding everyone's ear drums, wiping the *sang-froid* from lovely, refined faces.

And then, silence. Nobody budged, nobody breathed. One split second of stillness, hesitation, as if all the guests were actors on a stage, directed to freeze like mannequins for an instant. When that instant ended, panicked people stampeded toward the balcony, shouting, pushing, shoving, poking, cursing, crying, clutching, squeezing, grabbing for cellphones, spilling drinks and dropping food. *The Day of the Locust,* East Coast style.

"She threw herself off."

"Who was it?"

"She lost her balance."

"Oh my God."

"Sophia Frost."

"Someone call 911!"

"She was drunk."

"She was pushed."

"Impossible!"

"It was Sophia!"

"Sophia Frost?"

"I heard the body hit the pavement!"

"Oh God!"

The mob rushed out the front door to the sound of sirens blasting below, like a herd of frantic horses fleeing a burning stable. By the time most of the guests had vacated the apartment, the sirens had been shut off, and silence reigned once again.

"How could this happen?" Laurel whispered. The world was crumbling. Gradually her head found its way onto the shoulder of her consoling new acquaintance, an action that didn't seem improper given the harrowing, dizzying, life-and-death circumstance. Patrick's arms gently surrounded her, and Laurel's stomach dropped. "Do you know Sophia Frost?" she murmured into his shoulder.

"No. Do you?"

"No. But I've been on that balcony with Ophelia," Laurel sighed.

"Spectacular view, especially at night with all those lights below."

"I could be wrong," Laurel mused like a sleuth, "but I have a feeling it was the woman in burgundy. She seemed distressed about something."

"I didn't notice her."

"She touched my arm. *Gripped* it actually. I might still have her fingerprints on me."

"At least she didn't feel any pain."

"How do you know that?"

"The human body will fall at a speed faster than the brain can register pain."

"A smidgen of comfort in the chaos," Laurel breathed. "Do you suppose it was an accident?"

"Depends how troubled she was," Patrick replied. "The clinically depressed do jump from balconies."

"At festive birthday parties?"

"*Especially* at festive birthday parties," he emphasized. "I've treated some of them."

"You're a psychiatrist?"

"Psychologist," he said. "Everyone has a story."

She nodded, gently pulling away from Patrick, but remaining within range of his musky scent. He brought his wine goblet to Laurel's lips. The pinot noir was silky and rich, with a sweet, subtle edge. "Everyone does have a story," she agreed. "Earlier, I overheard a woman tell her husband, 'He *makes* things happen, Lance. You *let* them happen.' Obviously she thinks he's a wimp."

"Not only that," Patrick added, "but she knows another guy who's *not* a wimp."

"Lance wasn't a wimp his whole life," Laurel pointed out as if she knew the guy. "Over time he *turned into* one."

"People change, drift apart."

"Do they have to drift apart?" Laurel asked. "He might try to become stronger, more secure."

"You can't change to suit someone else," Patrick asserted with professional conviction. "It's a lesson people learn too late. Let's face it, Lance is a loser."

"Poor Lance," Laurel muttered. "Something else I overheard: A dignified man, maybe a professor or U.N. ambassador, plied an unsuspecting Girl Scout with gin gimlets."

Patrick stifled a laugh with a gulp of wine. "Well, let's not judge him too harshly. In all likelihood he was trying to get a free box of Girl Scout cookies. Who doesn't love those Thin Mints?"

The front door swung open, bringing silence to the room. A small group of guests entered with expressions so grim, so mournful, they might as well have just returned from a wake.

A few seconds later, Ophelia appeared, ashen. She addressed the crowd. "If you were on the balcony when Sophia fell, the police would like to speak with you. The party is officially over, but feel free to stay. I think it would be fitting to share a moment of silence in memory of our friend Sophia."

Eyelids closed and nobody dared to sneeze. The silence was thick and uncomfortable, like in a library. Visions of Sophia flooded Laurel's mind. She half opened her eyes and scolded herself for letting the woman go. She should've pulled her into the hallway and insisted on offering help.

"Thank you," Ophelia said.

All eyes opened to reveal faces whipped with sadness. A woman was dead.

Patrick brought his lips to Laurel's ear. "Would you like to continue our conversation someplace else?" he whispered.

"Um…yes," she said, grateful for the invitation. "First let me say goodbye to Ophelia."

"Take your time. I'll wait downstairs." He turned away and darted toward the front door. She watched his retreating figure and felt a slight disappointment that he didn't look back towards her with a smile or a small wave of the hand.

In the kitchen, Ophelia was surrounded by a circle of guests listening intently, almost with worship, to what she was saying. Laurel felt terribly sorry for her, the well-ordered precision of her party shattered by a gruesome suicide. The four-tiered, red velvet birthday cake, frosted in white fondant, remained on the table. Candles hadn't been lit, tributes hadn't been made. The fabulous Ophelia would turn forty only once, and the momentous birthday would be remembered for the wrong reason. Laurel decided to slip away silently without saying goodbye.

Outside, she was struck by the eerie tableau set before her eyes. Scores of onlookers stood on the sidewalk in stony silence, staring at the body in the gutter covered by a blanket. Blood seeped through. The street was cordoned off. Police officers roamed with flashlights, speaking in hushed tones. The unique scent of wet concrete hung in the air; a light rain had fallen. The atmosphere was apocalyptic, as if all those present had no place to go because their homes had been destroyed.

On the lookout for Patrick and for puddles, Laurel made her way through the crowd. She assumed he would appear from behind a cluster of people. When he didn't, she forged her way back to the front of Ophelia's building and leaned against the wrought iron gate, waiting for him to find her, certain he would show.

Two minutes turned to five, five became ten. The dread was rising, unrelenting, every second chipping away at Laurel's mountain of hope until it was reduced to a hill, then a knoll, a protuberance, and finally a mound of wet mud. The six-footer with the seductive eyes had departed, disappeared, *disintegrated* for all she knew. Maybe he wasn't even real.

Laurel couldn't stop herself from devising one plausible scenario after another. Did he meet someone else on the way down? Was he stuck in one of the building's four elevators? Maybe he was looking for a polite way to extricate himself because he was engaged. Or bisexual. Bipolar. Bionic. Maybe was playing some kind of cruel game in which he flirted with a woman, then hit the road. Whatever the reason, she intended to delete him from her mind like Gmail spam.

Twenty maddening, mystifying minutes after leaving the party, it was time to call it a night, a horrendous one. Baffled and crestfallen, Laurel began walking south. She passed two diminutive elderly ladies. "Couldn't she have just taken the elevator?" one of them asked the other with absolute sincerity.

Laurel couldn't help laughing. Then the bright white beam of a policeman's flashlight struck her face, startling and embarrassing her. "I'm sorry," the officer said, redirecting his light. "Didn't mean to blind you."

"Uh, OK," she stuttered. "Is there something you want?"

"You're dressed like you were at the party in the penthouse, and I'm wondering if you knew Sophia Frost."

"No. I didn't."

"Oh. All right," he muttered. "Sorry about the light."

"I'm over it."

"You look nice, by the way."

"Thanks," Laurel responded, stunned. She looked more closely at the officer. He had the kind of face that always needed a shave, and his thick black hair always needed a trim. At another time, in a different place, she might have offered to look for a pair of scissors. The guy wasn't bad looking.

"Well, have a good night," he said.

A good night? Not only was it one of the worst nights in recent memory, Laurel figured it was the odds-on favorite to take top honors for the worst of the year. "You too, officer."

"Eric," he said.

"Eric," she responded with a faint smile. She continued her slow walk south.

Neither the surprise flirtation nor the flashlight in the face had prepared Laurel for the night's next shock. Her hand covered her open mouth, and she froze.

Standing ten or twelve feet away was the emaciated stranger in the backless burgundy dress. The active ghost of Sophia Frost. Laurel remained irresolute, her hand still over her mouth. Just to make sure this wasn't some hallucination brought on by two flutes of champagne, one sip of wine, a tiny valium and a splash of vodka, she took a few tentative steps toward the apparition. There was no question that the provocative dress was the same. And the bony, exposed back couldn't have possibly belonged to anyone else.

The living-dead creature turned to Laurel. "We met at the party," Laurel quickly said, the words faltering in her throat. "Ophelia Gimble's. *Gamble's,* I mean."

"I was there, yes," she replied in a warm, husky voice.

"We didn't exactly meet, but you used my arm to get your balance, remember? Well, that's beside the point. I'm…I'm just so glad to see you." Carried along by a surge of emotion, she threw her arms around this bag of bones. Then, she took a sudden step back, hoping her spontaneous embrace wasn't inappropriate or unwelcome. "I'm very sorry," she gushed, wiping a tear away. "Please forgive me. It's just that...".

"Yes," the stranger interrupted, nodding in a knowing way. "Emotions are running high."

"Off the chart actually." Now that Laurel had a chance to study her, she realized this slender woman was as beautiful as she was offbeat: pale green eyes, plump magenta lips, perfectly sculpted nose, and cascading hair the color of pomegranate juice. She appeared so wispy that Laurel was afraid she'd vanish into thin air if she looked away. "Did you know Sophia Frost?" Laurel asked.

"I did," she shared with a surprising nonchalance that suggested she was bored with the subject.

"I didn't know her at all," Laurel replied.

"You're so much better off. She was a complicated mess." There was a hint of an accent – something European – that gave this wafer-thin woman an aura of elegance and intellectualism, like she might've been Simone de Beauvoir in a past incarnation. "She once proclaimed that death would set her free. Imagine having breakfast with someone who says that while munching on French toast. Free from *what?* She had a divine life. Lance was a devoted husband."

"Lance?" Laurel said. "Of course. Lance was at the party."

"The bitch dragged him everywhere."

"How is he holding up?"

"How would *you* hold up if your spouse jumped off a balcony? But he'll bounce back in time, like Paris after the Franco-Prussian War."

"Right," Laurel nodded. "The woman must've been in a lot of pain."

"The woman *was* a lot of pain. Pain personified, that's what the woman was." She took her time lighting a cigarette. She tossed the match in the air.

"How do you know Ophelia?" Laurel asked.

"We met at the foot of Mount Kilimanjaro."

"Of course you did. I'm Laurel Finnegan, by the way."

"Ah," she responded with approval. "Finnegan. Not Laura but Laurel. Unique. My birth name is Gina. However, people refer to me as the Countess. That's what I'm called." Her swanlike neck fell back so that she could gaze at the sky.

"Are you a real countess?" Laurel asked.

"No. Tomorrow I'm having a few people over for coffee and Scrabble," she said, lowering her eyes to focus on Laurel, "so I invited Sophia and Lance. She told me they couldn't make it because they were catching a midnight train to Athens, Georgia."

"A midnight train to Georgia?" Laurel inquired with a half-smile.

"Official departure time was eleven forty." She took a drag of her cigarette, exhaling a cloud of smoke and watching it billow. "You have to understand that Sophia was a pathological liar. We all tell a harmless fib now and again, but this slag lied about everything: her childhood, finances, diet, sex life. She *enjoyed* lying, like some people enjoy tennis, or scrapbooking."

"My God."

"It was a pastime, a sport. Do you like these shoes?" the Countess asked, lifting her leg to display her leopard suede pumps. "Too dark to see. Excuse me!" she called out to Eric. "Could you point your big wand over here please?" Eric pointed his flashlight at her foot. "Thank you. Designed by an orthopedic surgeon named Rose, so they're good for the feet, and very stylish." She exhibited more enthusiasm about her shoes than she did about her deceased acquaintance. The Countess returned her foot to the ground but the spotlight remained. "Enough!" she shouted to the officer. "Unless you want to try them on."

"I see him in more of a white strappy sandal," Laurel whispered.

"Can I help you with anything else, ladies?" he asked.

"Not right now but thank you, Eric," Laurel tossed back. He

looked her up and down before stepping away. Laurel bit her lip.

"Do you know this man?" the Countess inquired.

"Not really. He introduced himself before."

"His eyes are magical for such a masculine face."

"I didn't notice," Laurel replied. "He'll probably want to talk to you since you knew Sophia."

"I'll be going upstairs. I'm sure there will be police to talk to." The Countess took another drag of her cigarette. "Who knows? Maybe death *will* set her free as a gull flying over the shore." She scanned the dark, infinite sky. "Maybe we'll be lucky and she'll fly into a lighthouse."

Laurel said nothing as the face of the Countess changed dramatically. Her eyes closed, lips quivered. Nostrils flared and breathing became heavy. She tried to say something, but words didn't emerge. A nod of the head acknowledged something to someone, maybe someone far away, maybe herself. "Lance is a prince," she finally managed to utter. "I don't know a soul who doesn't love him, including myself."

Laurel was taken aback by this unexpected outburst from a woman who offered a first impression of being frozen. "You're in love with him," she breathed, watching the pain roll across the Countess's face.

"When he married that ogre, I couldn't rouse myself from bed for a month. I was physically sick with love, paralyzed. He said he loved me too, but he married *her*."

"That must've been devastating."

"For a time. It might've been *me* who hurled myself off a balcony. Nobody could figure out what he saw in her. I drove myself mad with that puzzle."

"What was your conclusion?" Laurel asked.

"Love doesn't play by rules," she stated. "Write that down

and frame it. There's no rational explanation why somebody loves somebody else. It defies science, logic, reason. There's no way to make it start, no way to make it stop."

Laurel nodded with understanding. "I hear that."

"And then," she said, "time plays a trick. Time, often a friend, can completely change a situation. Lance fell in love with me and decided to leave her. He finally saw her for what she is. Was."

"Amazing."

"And he told her at Ophelia's party. I warned him not to. Wrong time, wrong place. She was as insecure as a wooden bridge in a windstorm. But Lance does what he wants, even if a potential repercussion is death." She took what was left of her cigarette and tossed it to the ground. "I should go back to him."

"All right." Laurel took a moment to snap a picture in her mind, a detailed shot of this bizarre, world-weary, much-too-lean, but very much alive, woman whose feelings ran deeper than they seemed. "When did Lance realize he was in love with you?"

"One month ago. Sophia was in a Scandinavian asylum and Lance took me on a tour of the fjords in Northwestern Norway. An ideal place for love, don't you agree?"

"Uh, yes," Laurel hesitated.

"You've seen the fjords?"

"Uh, no."

"You must," she insisted. "When the right time comes, in the right place, you need to act immediately because the next time might be horribly wrong."

"I understand. And time moves so quickly."

"One day you're born, the next you turn thirty, the next you turn sixty. And the next? I don't have to tell you."

Laurel took a deep, slow breath. "Maybe we'll meet again before we turn sixty, under different circumstances."

"More likely we won't, but stranger things have happened just in the last hour." The Countess turned and strolled away as a cool breeze accompanied her. No hugs, no goodbyes.

Laurel stood her ground and watched the retreating figure. It was the last thing she expected, but before disappearing into the darkness, the Countess turned back and waved a small regal wave. Laurel's eyes welled with tears.

As she began to drift south, the sounds of cars, conversation, music, and beer cans rattling against the curb combined to create a cacophonous, uplifting urban melody.

Tooth Decay

BEFORE THE CURIOUS SERIES OF EVENTS that left his quiet community stunned, Calvin Flack, DDS wondered if he would ever find the perfect dental hygienist.

Two weeks prior to opening his practice in picturesque Whitefish Bay, Wisconsin, the soft-spoken dentist hired Solange Chaucer, a strawberry blonde with a subtle overbite. Solange performed her duties expertly, but one morning Calvin caught her using nitrous oxide for recreational purposes. He was so outraged and disappointed that someone would take advantage of the profession he revered, he fired her on the spot. The flustered hygienist had nothing to say in her defense; she simply packed her personal items and left the premises, laughing all the way.

After hiring, then soon firing, Donna Zeigdansky who refused to wear a standard white uniform because it wasn't "her color" (she dressed in black, which unnerved some patients), Imogene Jackson, office manager and drill sergeant, escorted Rosalie Sterling into Calvin's immaculate office. A silky-haired stunner with voluptuous breasts, Rosalie reminded Calvin of a refreshing summer dessert. Not only did she display chalk-white teeth, glowing gums, and impeccable posture (as if she could balance a hardcover copy of *Dental Anatomy* on her head while walking), she boasted degrees from Vassar, the Sorbonne, and the University of Wisconsin at Stout. Her vast knowledge of periodontics was as impressive as her ability to speak fluent French, German, and Farsi.

"I like your office," Rosalie said. "And your teeth."

"Thank you. The style is New England," he told her. "The office, not my teeth."

"Yes," she said with a sparkling smile.

He scrutinized her, silently auditing her flaws. There were none. "When did you first become interested in dentistry?"

Rosalie explained that she had always enjoyed putting her fingers in people's mouths. As a young girl, she giggled at the warm, wet feel of teeth and tongue. As a teenager, a human mouth was a mysterious cave, a complex, intriguing region begging for exploration. Even as an adult, she loved to slip on a plastic glove and probe inner cheeks. Overwhelmed by Rosalie's interest in all things oral, and ecstatic that he found someone as fascinated with tooth care as *he* was, Calvin offered her the position on the spot. He missed her already, and she was still there.

Imogene was proud of herself for discovering Rosalie. She'd perused more than two hundred resumes of recent dental school graduates before scheduling appointments with just three candidates. Of the three, Rosalie had the most thorough training. Plus, she had just moved to Whitefish Bay and didn't know a soul. This worked in her favor because Imogene desperately wanted to forge new friendships after ending her ten-year association with Jo Marie Gurwitch. Jo Marie had accused Imogene of harboring romantic feelings for Dr. Flack, and this was simply not acceptable.

The first question Imogene asked Rosalie on her first official workday was an unexpected one. "Do you have a boyfriend?"

"Not at the moment," she replied. "I just moved here from Ipswich."

"Calvin is married, you realize," Imogene stringently stated. "His wife, Hedda, is the head of Housekeeping at the Whitefish Bay Elegance Hotel."

"Any children?" The question squirted out of her mouth like toothpaste from a full tube.

"They've been trying and trying, but so far no luck. They're giving it another six months before resorting to radical fertilization procedures." Rosalie was startled to hear such personal, unrequested information. "Hedda took me to lunch last month," Imogene said with a peculiar sense of pride. "She was impressed that I carried a bottle of mint mouthwash in my tote."

"Who *wouldn't* be?"

Imogene flashed Rosalie a wide grin. "Would you like to smell my breath?" she asked.

"Could I take a rain check?"

"You betcha," Imogene responded. "It rains around here a lot, you know. That's Roxanne," she announced, pointing to a smudgy framed photo of a Siamese cat displayed on her desk. "She's a little bit pregnant."

"Sweet," Rosalie responded with a strained smile, concluding that this woman was a strange bird, one that should probably be extinct.

To Imogene, Dr. Flack was a pure-bred, perfect-toothed prince, but she considered her feelings strictly platonic. She also knew the dentist didn't think of her in any way except as a loyal office manager, and he *wouldn't* think of her in any other way until she lost sixty pounds, did something with her mess of red hair, and had the oval mole on her neck removed. Sometimes Imogene would think about her dentist-prince as she drifted off to sleep, and he would invariably make an appearance in a dream, often in his crisp white uniform, sometimes only in sky blue boxers.

"When's the next appointment?" Calvin asked Rosalie late one morning during her third week.

"Not till two-thirty," she told him. "Wes Codling cancelled."

"How does lunch at Gopher Bar & Grill sound?"

"Sounds like a plan," she purred. Gopher Bar & Grill, with its gorgeous view of Whitefish Bay's colorful lily garden, was one of the top two restaurants in town. The other, Dipsy Lime, only served dinner.

At Gopher, smartly-dressed patrons crowded the hostess stand, eagerly waiting to be seated. The scent of sizzling pork permeated the place, making mouths water and stomachs gurgle. Calvin and Rosalie were led to a deep leather banquette next to a pink fabric wall where two menus and tall glasses of water were waiting. After perusing the specials, a spiky-haired waiter named Finn took their food order. The cumin-crusted sturgeon with yucca puree, poached quail egg and banana fingerling potatoes tempted Calvin, but he went with the T-bone steak. Rosalie was in the mood for the veal shank with saffron cream sauce but opted for a small cucumber salad.

When the waiter left the table, a cloud of sexual tension hung in the air. Calvin couldn't deny an intense attraction to Rosalie. He could hardly wait to arrive in the office every morning and watch her float from room to room, performing her job duties with the utmost professionalism. Rosalie's smile was infectious, and her mysterious scent intoxicating. Sometimes Calvin actually envied his patients, able to sit back in the comfortable chair, open their mouths, and let Rosalie's fingers in. He was beyond smitten. He'd never felt this way, not even during the early, heady days with Hedda.

"It's astonishing that the majority of people have some form of gum disease, don't you think?" Rosalie asked as she fiddled with her silverware.

Calvin nodded. "Eighty per cent of the population. Imagine."

"I know." Her eyes grew wide. "Not sixty, not seventy."

"Eighty."

They contemplated this astronomical number, allowed it to sink in.

"You know what irks me?" Rosalie asked. "Most people don't realize that inflammation of the gums due to plaque can lead to a build-up of plaque in the arteries."

"Which can obviously lead to a heart attack."

"Exactly."

"Do you know what they say, whoever they are?" Calvin inquired. "Dentists have the highest rate of suicide of any profession. I've never thought about ending it all, have *you?*"

"Oh no. Never understood that. I'm having a great time."

"Me too. We get to take care of people's teeth and make a living at it."

"I feel the same way."

"We should count our blessings."

"Absolutely."

All too soon, the dentist's expression turned serious. "Come to think of it," he said, "a dentist friend of mine hung himself. Dean Crookshank."

"Oh my God," Rosalie gasped. "That's awful. Actually, one of my classmates in dental school slit her wrists during sophomore year. It was the talk of the campus."

"Did she die?"

"Yes. She lost gallons of blood. But it's not like dentistry is the only field with suicide. I'm sure the automotive industry has its share."

"Undoubtedly."

"Want to hear something wild? In Kale County, an oral surgeon jumped off the roof of a building downtown. Plunged five stories to his death. Believe it or not, his name was Laszlo Molar."

Rosalie merely shook her head, mystified. "Molar," she whispered.

The entrees were delivered, and the duo immediately dug in. They devoured their lunches in record time. Almost as soon as their plates were empty, Finn appeared with dessert menus.

"No dessert for us," Calvin announced without conferring with Rosalie.

"Coffee?"

"Not for me," Calvin replied. "Stains the teeth."

"I'll pass, too," Rosalie said.

When they returned to the office, Imogene was rustling dental insurance forms on her disheveled desk. "How was lunch?" she asked perfunctorily.

"Excellent," Rosalie said.

"Their food is to die for," Calvin added as he hurried down the hall.

"Well," Imogene barked, "my Swiss cheese on pumpernickel was tasty, even though I was so frantic to get out of the house this morning that I forgot mayo, and I love mayo. I should've asked you to bring back a small tub."

"I would've been happy to," Rosalie said. "Why didn't you call my cell?"

"Didn't want to disturb you," Imogene said, in a voice like ice on sensitive teeth. "May I ask what you had for dessert?"

"Skipped dessert. We didn't want to be away from the office too long." She paused, noticing a half-eaten piece of peach pie sitting on a napkin. "Plus, I'm on a diet. Four's the new six, you know."

"Then you should've ordered *in*," Imogene suggested, ignoring the last comment, having been a size twelve most of her life. She grabbed her fork and jabbed the peach pie as if poking an eye. "I have menus from everywhere," she said around a mouthful of pie. "Look."

She grabbed a half dozen paper menus from her desk drawer and brandished them in front of Rosalie. "Piero's Pizza, Burger Haven, Crab Palace. Olive Garden too."

"I'll remember that," Rosalie responded before vanishing down the hall.

The following afternoon, Calvin and Rosalie were performing Myrtle Cash's root canal when Imogene gently knocked on the door. "Roxanne's gone into labor," she said in a loud whisper. "I have to rush home. If anyone wants a kitten, let me know."

Twenty minutes later, work on Myrtle Cash was complete. Calvin was proud of the job he did, though it wasn't his greatest achievement. That honor went to his porcelain-fused-to-gold-alloy crown on Smilla Hohenstein. The next patient wasn't due for a half hour, so Calvin and Rosalie found themselves alone in the cozy examination room. The previous day's conversation, specifically how death in dentistry hovered over every cleaning, filling, and wisdom tooth extraction, hung in the air like a bad case of halitosis. "Would you do me a favor?" Calvin asked.

"Of course," she replied.

Calvin hesitated momentarily. Then he blurted, "Floss my teeth?"

Rosalie lit up. "It would be my pleasure."

Calvin stretched out on the dental chair while Rosalie stood behind him. She flossed carefully, one upper tooth after the next, dislodging all unwanted food particles. Then the dentist rinsed. In order to plunge at his bottom set, Rosalie stepped to the side of the chair. With Olympiad flexibility, she flung her leg over Calvin's torso, straddling him off the ground. He held his breath. Then she went to work on his bottom teeth as the blood tingled through both their bodies.

After Rosalie finished flossing and Calvin finished rinsing, neither budged. The devoted dental professionals indulged in ardent conversation about creative tongue treatment, periodontal disease prevention, and innovative bleaching procedures. Surrounded by suction hoses and sinks, shiny metal instruments and mouthwash, the sexual tension that had been building for weeks finally broke when Calvin rested his hand on Rosalie's exposed thigh and slid a finger upwards. Very soon their clothing was on the floor as Rosalie bounced and bobbed. The dark leather dentist chair emitted squeaks and moans as did the dental couple. Rosalie swooped down for the occasional kiss like a seagull diving for food.

The schedule fell smoothly into place: after Imogene went home at the end of the day, Calvin locked the office door, then he and Rosalie slipped into the examination room where she flossed him.

One week into the clandestine affair, Imogene felt a change in the air. She couldn't put her finger on it, so she called the dentist's wife for a friendly chat to see if she could sense anything. Worried that he was working too hard, Hedda expressed concern about her husband's long hours.

"Well," Imogene replied, "it's true. He's very hard at work. But that's because he's so dedicated."

"Has there been an epidemic of cavities?"

"Cavities are *always* on the rise in our sugar-coated culture, honey. May I ask a personal question?"

"Of course."

"How often do you floss?"

"Two or three times a week," Hedda told her.

"Do it once a day, dear," Imogene offered. "Men stay married to women with good teeth and vibrant gums."

"You're a living doll. Let's have lunch again soon."

"How's Thursday?" Imogene asked.

"Uh, next week would be better. Let's chat on Monday and we'll figure it out."

The following Friday evening, Imogene arrived home after a particularly frustrating day at the office - a parade of rude, filthy-mouthed patients. A nagging curiosity chipped away at her. After feeding her feline babies, she marched outside and climbed back into her dented Dodge Avenger.

As the sun set in broad, violet strokes across the immense sky, Imogene barreled down Jonquil Boulevard, scowling all the way. She parked a block from the office, and hauled her heavy body out of the vehicle.

Imogene grunted down the street. Her legs seemed to weigh a ton. "If size four is the new six, what's size twelve – the new twenty?" she muttered with disgust. She lifted her hand and caressed the mole on the side of her neck. "And then there's *this* horror show. The damn thing's the size of Utah. Removing it would be painful as childhood. I mean childbirth. Child frigging birth." A concerned nun listened to Imogene as she roared past. "What the blazes would he do without me? His size four whore would have to run the practice and then there goes the neighborhood."

Imogene silently, furtively let herself back into the office as disturbing sounds floated over her desk directly into her head. She moved down the dim, carpeted hallway to investigate. With each step, the gasps and groans grew more savage. Imogene braced herself. Then, with a quivering hand she flung the door open, revealing the lustful couple on top of the leather chair.

In two dizzying seconds, three sets of eyes formed a debauched circle of deceit, rage, and abandonment. Everything became so clear so quickly. The devastation in Imogene's face was obvious. Both Calvin and Rosalie were instantly inanimate.

Imogene forced herself to step toward them. When she stood close enough to smell Rosalie's floral perfume, she smacked the woman across the face, breaking a front tooth. Then she brought her lips to Calvin's cheek, kissed it gently, and moved to his mouth where she kissed him with passion.

Blood trickled down Rosalie's chin onto Calvin's bare stomach, as Imogene stomped out of the room. She grabbed an empty file box from the floor and loaded it with her personal belongings. Arms shaking, she wobbled out the front door and out of the office of Calvin Flack DDS, certain she would find another brilliant, charismatic dentist in need of her unique services.

Recollections of Miss Linley

The morning began like any other Friday, even though there was a certain kind of electricity in the air. To be honest, I barely slept the night before, but I didn't tell that to my second-grade students. What I told them was that they would be witnessing a very special, very significant event. How could I have possibly known we were about to be pasted into a page of history?

I lived four miles east of Lakeland Starr Elementary School. Every morning at seven-thirty, Monday through Friday, I caught a ride with my friend and colleague Jocelyn Cook who taught third grade at the same school. She lived two blocks from me and loved to tool around in her snazzy, cherry-red Studebaker convertible. I, on the other hand, was an abnormally nervous driver and would grab any excuse to avoid getting behind the wheel.

Jocelyn idolized the British model Jean Shrimpton and spent much too much time trying to copy her sophisticated, cutting-edge style. She dressed the way the Shrimp dressed (that was the model's nickname, the Shrimp) and applied her make-up in the same bold fashion. One morning Jocelyn pulled her hair into a side ponytail because that's how the Shrimp had been photographed for Life magazine. On our drive to school, I warned her this style could be deemed inappropriate for the classroom. (I didn't share the fact that it was inappropriate for any female over fifteen, Miss Shrimpton excepted.) Sure enough, our conservative principal Mr. Frischling called her into his office. Five minutes later, she zoomed into the faculty lounge to restyle the 'do.

On that special November morning, it wasn't Jocelyn who dressed like she was heading to a rare, unique event. It was *me* who put on a white Chanel suit with white gloves and a strand of pearls given to me by my father on my twenty-first birthday. I also wore two silver bracelets, and I slipped into a pair of brand new, gorgeous nineteen dollar patent leather pumps. "Good morning, Miss Cook," I chirped in the voice of a third grader as I climbed into Jocelyn's car. (This was our daily ritual.) She responded with a childlike, "Good morning, Miss Linley," a smoldering cigarette dangling from her ruby lips. Then she added, in her adult voice, "You don't figure on walking eleven blocks in those heels, *do* you, hon?" I hadn't thought about potential foot pain. When we got to school, I discarded my heels and changed into a pair of flats I kept in the classroom closet.

Jocelyn and I were the only teachers planning to take their students on a field trip that autumn day. We were joined by six additional adults (three for each class). The parents of every student had signed a consent slip, and the kids, of course, relished any excuse to take a break from book reports and science projects.

At 11:30, we clustered in front of the school building. The weather was fine: sunshine, warm breeze, a few clouds in the sky. (It had drizzled earlier in the morning but no more rain was expected.) After breaking into small groups (four students and one adult), we held hands while briskly strolling down one block after the next. Clusters of Texans excitedly rushed alongside us, behind us, in front of us. In the distance, I could see a sizeable crowd gathering. "Hold hands tightly," I admonished the kids.

We were getting close to Dealey Plaza; that's when the adrenaline started to pump. By the time we arrived, hundreds had lined up along Elm Street, many carrying cameras, some with babies in tow. Jocelyn and I parked our groups under a large tree where we would have a clear view of the President of the United States as his car passed by.

We huddled together, enjoying the smell of freshly mowed grass hanging in the air like a mist. At exactly 12:30, the energy around us dramatically changed, as if some seismic event had occurred. All eyes turned left, and the motorcade came into view. The first car we saw was a white Ford occupied by four brawny men. Following the Ford was a black Lincoln Continental convertible. In the back seat, unmistakably, were Jack and Jackie. What struck me was the president's hair, his not-quite-brown hair that in the bright afternoon sunlight took on a reddish glow, almost crimson. Even from a distance I could see President Kennedy smiling. Jackie sat as the epitome of elegance in her rose pink suit and pillbox hat. All too soon there was another car, then another, then another. The president had disappeared from our sight, but his magic lingered.

When the first shot rang out, I thought it was a firecracker. Nothing more than an annoyance. Then the second one came, followed by the third. It only took another second for the reality to sink in. Jocelyn grabbed my arm. "What just happened?" she shrieked.

My first impulse was to yell, "Get down, everyone! Down on the ground!"

People began running in all directions like horses set free from a burning stable. "The president was shot!" a woman shouted. I felt as if I'd been punched in the stomach by Sonny Liston.

"We have to get them out of here," Jocelyn whimpered.

"Everyone, listen carefully," I shouted. "We're going to stand up and walk very fast, holding hands. Is that clear?" The sea of little heads, their eyes glowing with trust and obedience, nodded up and down.

The long trek back was strenuous and emotional. Strangers on the street were sobbing. Some leaned against stores and buildings in stunned silence. When one street was behind us, another loomed ahead. With aching ankles I surged along, adrift in a sea of concrete. I didn't stop to light a cigarette like Jocelyn did with an unsteady hand. My necklace threatened to choke me. Without missing a step, I removed it and put it in my purse along with my bracelets.

When our school finally revealed itself, a blur of brick and glass in the distance, it appeared as a fuzzy mirage. A scattering of adults darted in and out of the building; those coming out were holding the hands of small children. Mr. Frischling, waiting for us on the wide front steps, appeared wan and shaken. "We've called all parents and we're sending the children home," the principal said, his voice cracking and eyes rimmed red.

Life took a hairpin turn on that November afternoon and proceeded in an uncomfortable new direction. If the world had been viewed in pleasing, pretty soft-focus, now the picture was raw and brutally frank. We never talked about any of it. In 1963, the term *post-traumatic stress disorder* didn't exist. But we were all afflicted, every one of us who woke up that morning, made our way over to Elm Street and witnessed history.

I finished out the school term. Then I moved north, took a teaching job in Seattle. I didn't wait for Dallas to reclaim its bold, proud identity. I'd already lost some of my own.

In 1970, I married Daniel Sloan. My students called me Mrs. Sloan but in my heart I was Miss Linley. Something inside me froze on that November day in '63. It stuck in time and would prevent me from moving forward in a complete way. I would always be a little anxious about what each morning had in store. I knew it was possible for a beautiful day to turn dark and ugly in the blink of an eye.

Jocelyn and I kept in touch for a time. A letter every few months segued into a letter once a year, and they got progressively incoherent. She married a stockbroker, then a doctor, then a businessman. Then she moved to Atlanta, then Charlotte, then Mobile, and that was the last I heard from her. Every Christmas I received a holiday card from Mr. Frischling. In December of 1984 he included a note inside the card, informing me that Jocelyn had taken her life. The news hit me hard.

I close my eyes and I'm there. I can feel the warm air and smell the grass. I see the clustering, smiling people; I hear the shots and watch their smiles turn to confusion and then horror. Then I open my eyes and remind myself how many decades it's been, and I wonder if anyone else relives that afternoon with such gut-wrenching clarity. I wonder if anyone else dreads November the way I do.

The Mourners Wore Magenta

ALTHOUGH THE LUNGS OF THE MUMFORD PATRIARCH were clearing, and the granulomas were no longer blocking his fragile esophagus, he decided to pull the plug. Ninety-five years was plenty of time on this planet, he figured. He would leave two daughters and several grandchildren behind, as well as a curiously large number of female acquaintances.

On this humid July morning, more than one hundred forlorn friends and relatives filtered into the small, stuffy church to pay their respects to Bartholomew Mumford. The combined perfumes of the women in attendance, who outnumbered the men 2-to-1, thickened in the sweltering heat, sending more than one mourner to the restroom, queasy and wobbling.

The now-orphaned Lizzy felt lost and grief-stricken. Her estranged sister Cheyenne showed up with her soon-to-be-ex-husband Serge and their two daughters.

"When one attends a funeral, isn't one supposed to dress in black?" Cheyenne whispered into Serge's ear as a summer shower began to spatter the roof.

"I thought so," he responded.

"Then why are those women in the back wearing pink?" A cluster of heavily hairsprayed females between the ages of thirty and sixty were sitting in the last pew. All were dressed in various shades of pink, from coral to magenta. Cheyenne raised her eyebrows and shook her head.

The middle-aged priest with thin lips and a rubbery neck spoke eloquently of Bart Mumford, his devotion to family as well as his solid work ethic. "He didn't attend church regularly," the priest intoned, "but when he did, you always knew he was there." Suddenly, rain slammed down, drowning the priest's squeaking voice. "He was an independent thinker as well as a respected scholar," he shouted. A woman in the fifth pew began to gag before standing up and scurrying out a side door. "Now it's time to hear a few cherished memories of Bart Mumford from those who knew him best."

Lizzy spoke first, delivering the loving words everyone expected to hear. Cheyenne followed, emphasizing the enormous generosity of her father who had donated hundreds of thousands of dollars to various medical centers and aquariums.

Then one of the women from the rear pew, a chestnut-haired beauty in a silk magenta dress, strolled up and clutched the lectern. She took a moment to peruse the crowd before identifying herself as Sylvia Bleiweiss. "We've heard such wonderful words about Bart Mumford," Sylvia said. "He was certainly well-educated. We met at an aquarium function, and he immediately impressed me with his knowledge of marine mammal mating rituals. Not only did he teach me the sex habits of spotted sea trout, he explained how water temperature can influence the desires of certain female fish." Lizzy glanced at Cheyenne, startled, and gasps bubbled through the stale air. "Then he invited me for a midnight swim in a nearby lake. The light of the full moon created the most romantic setting imaginable. We went back to that lake every night for a week. On the final night, as I waded in the warm, soothing water, he swam ashore, got dressed, and vanished. Along with my clothes."

Sylvia left the podium abruptly, as if late for a bus. A sultry brunette in a beaded salmon-colored suit took the stage. "I'm Lana Prawn," she announced in a rich, creamy voice. "Bart and I met in Barbados. He wined me, dined me, and took me skinny-dipping on our second date. Did you know the female swordtail fish matures faster sexually when she encounters a male with a larger than average tail?" The church was silent. Cheyenne looked ill. "We had a splendid, magical time," Lana explained. "Then he dumped me on the beach at sunset, just left me there, threw me back into the sea like a sick guppy. The man had the conscience of smoked sturgeon."

By this time, the mourners were sitting on the edge of their pews. Lana strolled off, and because the rain had stopped, the only sound was the clacking of her stilettos on the hardwood floor.

A lively, silver-haired gal hurried to the stage in a hot pink prairie dress complete with matching boots, more appropriate for a square dance than a funeral. "I met Bart on the beach at sunset, right after he dumped Lana Prawn," the woman announced. "Of course I didn't know that at the time. Before long, I learned three things about Bart: He wore too much Old Spice, he considered the aquarium a kind of church, and he insisted I put on a swimsuit and hand wash his big black Mercedes while Peggy Lee played in the background. Kind of strange, I know. But I thought he was a good guy. Then one Sunday, we took a leisurely drive up the coast. He pulled into a service station to fill up on gas and buy a bag of chips, so I used the opportunity to run to the loo. When I came out, the Mercedes was gone. At first I was sure he was playing a joke. But when three hours passed and he hadn't returned, I realized he left me there like the shell of a spicy shrimp. I never heard from the bastard again. And I'd washed that damn car that very morning."

One after the next, the parade of brightly-dressed ex-girlfriends clattered across the floor and shared their personal memories of Bart Mumford as Lizzie and Cheyenne listened in disbelief.

Following Fiona Dunlap's diatribe about Bart's barbaric treatment of her at a Tampa seafood restaurant, all eyes fell upon Clarissa Sloat, a statuesque Swedish woman in a pale pink pants suit. "I liked sleeping with Bart, but I didn't enjoy being awake with him. He had a habit of degrading me," she explained in a pained voice. "He would slap me hard on the buttocks and order me to make a face like a blowfish." She paused. A tense, pulsating silence filled the church. "In the privacy of my bedroom I had no problem with this, but he began behaving in a crabby, sadistic manner in public. At my sister's wedding reception, he shoved me into the four-tiered wedding cake and told me I didn't deserve to be served dessert. I had to hold my mother back from attacking him with her motorized wheelchair." Dozens of jaws dropped, and remained that way. "For lunch, he liked me to hand feed him pieces of swordfish dipped in sweet liqueur. I warned him that too much seafood could cause mercury poisoning, but he told me he didn't mind resembling a thermometer." A few subdued chuckles rippled through the crowd. "Now I wish he'd come down with *any* kind of poisoning."

Unable to restrain herself another second, Cheyenne bolted up from her front row pew. "Enough!" she shouted. "This is a funeral, for fuck's sake! Not only do you look like giant bottles of Pepto-Bismol, your memories of my father are despicable. The man isn't here to defend himself, so we're only getting one side of your sleazy stories of subjugation. Please leave this sacred house of worship right now!" .

"Are you denying he did these things to us?" Clarissa asked. .

"I can stand here with confidence and deny being in denial," Cheyenne stated. "Now please honor my family and get the hell out of here."

In a strange, pink procession, the lovely women of Bart Mumford vacated the premises. Following them were dozens of darkly-dressed guests who wondered if they ever knew the deceased at all. For all intents and purposes, the service was over.

Lizzy and Cheyenne, both in a fog of bewilderment and anger, drifted toward one another like lost souls with no place to call home. "Do you suppose they were telling the truth?" Lizzy asked.

"I don't think a dozen women would make up similar stories," Cheyenne reasoned.

"But wouldn't we have known? Or suspected something?"

Cheyenne shook her head in resignation. "I don't know."

"Why did they have to go up there and ruin his memory? And why on earth did he pull that plug? He might've had another few years."

"He liked being in charge; that much we knew. He controlled every aspect of his life," Cheyenne explained. "I guess he wanted control of his death, too." She gently put her arms around her grieving sister. Lizzy began to sob on Cheyenne's bare shoulder. "He abandoned those women in the middle of nowhere. Imagine being left all alone in a strange place."

"To flounder there with no clothes," Lizzy said.

"A fish out of water."

"Green around the gills."

A chuckle emerged from Cheyenne but she instantly quashed it. "Daddy was a perverted misogynist," she admitted, wiping tears from her cheeks. "He was a nasty, shellfish man. I mean *selfish*." At this point, a wave of hysterical laughter erupted. Lizzy joined in the merriment.

Not two seconds later, Lizzy realized how inappropriate this behavior was. "No!" she cried. "It isn't the least bit funny."

"You're right. Our father has died. And before that, he humiliated these poor women, all so pretty in pink."

"He lured them in with his man-made bait," Lizzy said.

"And they fell for him hook, line, and sinker." Another burst of laughter erupted from the sisters.

"We have to stop," Lizzy insisted.

"You're right. No more," Cheyenne agreed. "At least he didn't have to tackle them."

"Cheyenne!"

"I'm sorry. No more, I promise."

The women composed themselves before heading into courtyard. Dark, ominous clouds, still hiding the sun, gradually moved across the sky as if they had a specific destination. The heat remained intense. Small clusters of people were chatting quietly and conspiratorially. Only two of the magenta women were still there, and the sisters approached them cautiously. "I'm sorry," Lizzie quietly said.

"We're so sorry," Cheyenne tenderly added. Then she took Lizzie's arm and led her away, wanting nobody's sorrow, pity or sympathy. She certainly didn't want empty consolation. And the thought of her or her sister exploding in laughter was unthinkable.

Neither sister had any idea what the universe had in store for them. Cheyenne couldn't have known she would meet her future mate standing in front of the living kelp forest at the Atlantic Aquarium, or that she would conceive her daughter in the dimly-lit hallway around the corner from the seahorse kingdom. Lizzy had no inkling she would marry the man who created the giant octopus exhibit in the Deep Reefs Gallery, or that the wedding would take place in the aquarium lobby.

All the formerly estranged sisters felt on this somber day, the day of their father's unforgettable fiasco of a funeral, was an oddly compelling connection to all things crustacean.

Intended Target

HE FOLLOWED HER SOUTH. On a cloudy afternoon in May, Callie entered Rachel's cozy, one-story brick house and saw maroon-colored blood trickling from the hallway onto the white carpet in the living room, resembling raspberry sorbet on a snow drift. The body lay on the hardwood floor in front of the bedroom, eyes open and pleading. Later it would be determined by forensic specialists that Rachel's death was caused by an acute subdural hematoma, or a "severe head injury". The back of Rachel's skull was bloody, her hair a coagulated rat's nest. Strands of dark hair and blotches of dried blood soiled the bare wall. It wouldn't take a criminologist to figure out that the killer repeatedly banged the life out of Rachel's head against the wall.

With no evidence of forced entry, the police suspected Rachel was acquainted with her intruder. All her possessions were left untouched: Fendi purse, cash, credit cards, flat-screen TV, iMac, DVD player, small crystal box of Krugerrands. Definitely no robbery. The police didn't dismiss Callie's theory about Lucas, but they had no concrete reason to arrest him or even question him. They didn't even have *circumstantial* evidence.

"How are you doing?" her friend Ben Schjeldahl asked Callie

one Sunday afternoon over Chinese food at a neighborhood restaurant.

"I feel like a landmine blew up in my face," Callie said.

"I know," he responded.

Callie accepted the fact that this brutal, untimely death had come to define her. She was no longer an elementary school teacher or a wife or even a daughter. She was Rachel's best friend, impermeable to the influence of well-meaning acquaintances who advised her to move on with her life. It felt as if Callie's sole purpose was to keep Rachel's memory alive and loved.

"I was at the market last week," Callie announced, "and Sue Bracewell happened to be in the bread section."

"Why do I know that name?" he asked.

"She worked with Rachel at the credit union."

"Oh, the blonde one."

"Right. With the high-pitched voice. She told me, 'You're taking the death really hard, aren't you.' I just stood there like an idiot. How do you take a death *easily*? Do you go out dancing? Get drunk? Make new friends so you can forget about the dead one?"

"Strange thing to say." With his fork, Ben leisurely pushed Lampang chow mien around on his plate.

"I grabbed the nearest sourdough loaf and bolted. Didn't even say goodbye." Callie mournfully gazed out the large window beside them. The sky was a massive gray dome, but the gloominess of the city didn't bother her. She preferred clouds to bright sunshine; it made her feel safe, guarded. "Do you ever get the feeling you're living inside a very large womb?" she asked.

"Uh, no," Ben chuckled. "Can't say that I do."

A strong wind whipped the trees, leaves moving in thick manes like hair in front of a blow dryer. Just then, tea arrived at the table in bone china, and Ben's thumbs were too thick to navigate the dainty handles of the cup. He struggled and struggled, finally deciding to cradle the cup between his two palms like a gorilla. Callie cracked a smile. Despite the lack of sunshine, this was the brightest part of her week.

Callie had fled Vancouver abruptly, less than a week after giving notice at the private school where she taught. Looking for a job in Seattle was something she put off indefinitely. With enough cash in her savings account for a year, making money was at the bottom of her priority list. Besides, she didn't think her morose, zombie-like mien would have potential employers fighting over her.

Ben was as lost as Callie, completely freaked out about the way Rachel died. "It would have been easier to take if she was surrounded by family and friends, or if she'd been in a hospital bed being cared for by professionals."

Ben shared this unsettling thought with Callie as they sipped peppermint tea on the creaking front porch of his small house. The porch steps were in danger of collapsing, and the sagging roof prevented the screen door from opening all the way.

"I have no doubt it was Lucas," Callie sighed. "If I hadn't moved here, Rachel might still be alive."

"Don't play that game. It's destructive," he told her. "And it's out of your hands."

"I have a feeling he's back in Vancouver." Life with Lucas, all eighteen months of it, was anything but magical. They'd fallen in love and became husband and wife impulsively, barely a month after meeting. This was extremely uncharacteristic of the first-grade teacher who had a reputation for being orderly and predictable, for studying the facts and reading the fine print before making any decision. In an uncensored moment of raw honesty, she once admitted to Rachel that she married quickly to prove she could *be* unpredictable, to illustrate the fact that she had a bold, spontaneous and carefree side crouching beneath the surface.

Callie had been startled to see her husband's interest in drugs accelerate. He repeatedly tried to convince her to take part and she repeatedly refused. Late one night Lucas actually shoved Callie's head onto the glass coffee table where the powder had been lined up with precision. The glass shattered, and a tiny piece lodged in Callie's forehead, leaving a small permanent scar. She wanted to keep Lucas in her past, chalk him up as a short-sighted, ludicrous and deadly mistake.

When a flash thunderstorm slammed the roof, Callie and Ben grabbed their mugs of tea and darted indoors. They settled on the low, baggy sofa, Callie languishing on one end and Ben sitting stiffly on the other. He clicked on the TV and channel surfed. Nothing interested him, so he remained on CNN and pressed mute. The unmistakable scent of rain wafted through the window screen.

In the half-light, Ben nervously moved toward Callie. She wondered if she should leave, but she saw the vulnerability in his eyes, and it broke her heart. She leaned over and wrapped her arms around him in weary surrender, offering herself like a gift. She closed her eyes and waited for the gentle kiss she knew would come.

They slowly stood up, entwined. Ben picked Callie up, her legs around him, navigating from the living room into the darkened hallway. Ben pressed her against the wall, leaning his torso heavily on her. This kiss was without a hint of tenderness – hard, hungry and passionate.

They fell into the wood-paneled cocoon of the bedroom where Callie's dress crumbled to the floor with Ben's sweatshirt. With fumbling hands and racing hearts, they fell onto the king-size bed, restraint abandoned. Callie and Ben kissed, licked, groped, losing each other in the height of passion and their devotion to Rachel. Ben dug into her and Callie arched up; each desperate to find a piece of their absent friend underneath the other's flesh.

Callie rolled her body toward the edge of the bed. "On the floor," she whispered into Ben's ear. Ben obliged, rolling them the last inch over the side of the bed. It was anything but graceful; they landed with a thud. "Are you OK?" Ben asked. Callie didn't answer, her body anchored to the red area rug, clutching him like a life raft.

His back was a smooth, strong flotation device, his head a boulder, his legs sturdy tree trunks. She pulled him closer, silently asking for his full weight on her body, desperate for him to devour her, to crush her and make her forget.

When it was obvious there was no turning back, Callie grabbed Ben's hands and firmly placed them on either side of her head. Then she slammed the back of her skull against the floor again and again. Brain-rattling blows. Stars sprung to life in her eyes.

"What are you doing?" Ben cried out with alarm, pulling his hands away as Callie continued to unravel below him. She grabbed his hands and forcefully put them where they were before, directly over her ears. Her slender hands clasped his large, callused ones as she continued to bang her head against the floor in a fast, deliberate rhythm. "No," he snapped, and he pulled his hands and self away from her, out of her. But Callie kept going without his assistance, increasing the power with each blow as if she wanted to knock her brain out of its skull. Ben looked panicked as Callie's head continued to pound the floor, her consciousness rushing toward oblivion. She stopped when the room started spinning. An ocean rushed in her ears.

When it was over, neither spoke. Rattled, Ben got up from the floor and disappeared into the bathroom. Callie, wrapped in a haze of physical satisfaction, had no desire to get up. She remained on the rug, drenched in warm sweat and blissful fatigue. The pleasure was a guilty one. She'd stolen it, she realized from under her fog of satisfaction.

It was one thing for Callie to rationalize her decision to have sex with Ben, but it was a very different story to wonder how Rachel would have felt about it. What kind of a friend *was* she to make love with her best friend's boyfriend? The ultimate betrayal. It simply wasn't done, not even if the friend was dead.

Half awake, only half alive, Callie favored the half that was dead, and she tried to lose herself in its peace. But the half that was alive began to ache with pain and thirst. *Damn needs of the body, she thought.* Still, she didn't budge.

When too much time had passed, Ben gently lifted Callie onto the bed. Eyes closed, she said nothing. Ben joined her on the sheets, hoping they would face each other. But Callie turned away from him. Baffled and confused, he moved his bulky body as close to her as possible without touching. The last thing he wanted to see was Callie climb off the bed and get dressed.

The late hour was a relief to Callie; she pretended to be asleep. Despite the coolness of her body language, there was no other place she wanted to be, there was no one else she wanted to suffer with. Even so, she felt incapable of looking Ben in the eye. Curled up in a semi-fetal position, Callie escaped into a deep sleep.

A few short hours later, she awoke to the sound of water hammering down on the tiled floor of the shower. Just when she was growing comfortable with the sound, the water pressure took a nose dive, like thick pouring rain morphing into a light drizzle. She rolled on the bed and caught a glimpse of the dress she'd been wearing the previous night. It was carefully draped over the back of a chair, and she wound up gazing at it with a combination of surprise and gratitude. The sight strangely moved her; it was obvious

Ben had taken the dress from the floor and arranged it on the chair as delicately as he could. She had never felt such a strong surge of appreciation.

Then she thought: it should have been *Rachel* lying in Ben's bed that morning, *Rachel* listening to the water in the shower. Instead, it was Callie on the rumpled sheet with its soothing warmth and masculine scent. She was alive by mistake. Living by accident. It was *Callie* who Lucas was looking for that terrible afternoon, not her friend.

Callie braced herself as she heard Ben's footsteps, the boom of a caveman approaching. She closed her eyes but the darkness didn't take her far enough away.

"Are you all right?" Ben asked.

It impressed Callie that he didn't pretend she might still be asleep. "Yes," she said, opening her eyes.

A blue bath towel was tied around Ben's waist, revealing a sizable tattoo on his shoulder blade. "How'd you sleep?" he asked, gently sitting down on the edge of the bed.

"All right, I guess," she replied. "I didn't notice your tattoo last night."

"You didn't look close enough," he told her. "I know that you *don't* have one anywhere. You hungry?"

Her stomach revolted. The notion of eating eggs and bacon and buttered toast was totally repellent at the moment. "No. Not at all."

"You're OK?" he asked.

"Yes, yes. How about you?"

"Fine. What I mean is..." he hesitated. "Does your head hurt? Do you need an aspirin or something?" Her deranged action, the demented banging of her head on the floor, was now center stage, under the harsh lights, primed for dissection.

"I don't need anything, but thanks," she sighed. "Comfortable mattress."

"Yeah, I like it…Uh, if you want to shower, I'll get you a fresh towel."

"In a little while."

"OK. Just let me know."　He couldn't stand the palpable awkwardness another second. "What was that all about?"

"I don't know," Callie confessed.

"Did you want to have Rachel's experience?"

"It wasn't a decision, Ben. It took on a life of its own. Or maybe a death."

"I would never, ever hurt you," he stated.

"I know that."　She forced a tender smile. "Would you be willing to forget this happened?　To never, ever mention it again?"

"Of course," he replied. "Anything you want."

"Thanks," she whispered.

"I won't give up on you," he said, "unless you want me to. I really hope you don't want me to."　Ben's face was full of hope.

She gazed into his wistful eyes. "I don't want you to," she told him.

Architectural Digestion

"DID YOU HEAR WHAT HAPPENED IN PLACID?" Mitzi's voice crackled through Ada's cellphone.

"No, what happened?" Her best friend's tone implied bad news.

Ada and Buddy had just piled into their big old red truck, eager to head out on their long-awaited wilderness vacation in the Smoky Mountains. She glanced at her husband of forty years with a worried expression and mouthed "Mitzi."

"There was a tornado," Mitzi managed to say.

"How bad?" Ada asked, a flush of horror rising into her throat.

"From what I hear, very bad." Mitzi lived in Flounder, one town west of Placid.

"Let me try to call Colin," Ada said, and hung up.

"What happened?" Buddy asked. The suspense in the truck had its own pulse. Before responding, Ada speed-dialed their son. "A tornado hit Placid. She said it was bad." Ada sighed, listening for the ring.

"Oh no," Buddy whispered as he shut his eyes for a few seconds.

"Can't get through," Ada declared. "Phone lines must be down."

"Try Margaret."

Unable to reach either Colin or his wife Margaret, Ada and Buddy decided to postpone their canoeing, kayaking, and whitewater-rafting. "Let's get on Route 9," Ada said. The couple embarked on the most agonizing ride of their lives – ninety miles to Placid. Luckily, their bags were packed and they were fully stocked up on snacks, water, chewing gum, and gas.

The news on the radio was sketchy; the only solid information was that a tornado had whipped in and destroyed a major portion of Placid. "Evidently," the announcer said in a shaky voice, "there was no warning. Not one dang word."

Ada and Buddy silently prayed for their son's safety as the announcer continued. "The mayor of Placid is on vacation in Waikiki, but he got wind of the tragedy, and he'll be flying back on the second flight home. In the meantime, the mayor of Pollutia, the sister city of Placid, has offered his support and services." As Buddy drove, he reached over and took Ada's hand.

Buddy and Ada Klock met when they were both nineteen, and almost five decades later, white-haired and slightly withering, they remained inseparable. They were like a pair of comfortable old shoes. The leather was slightly torn, the color had faded, and the laces had entwined, forming knots that couldn't be untied. It was highly unusual for anyone in the small town of Honeycrisp to see either of them without the other.

Ada tried Colin again. Still no luck. She tried every few minutes. Buddy cleared his throat to speak, but Ada beat him to it. "Please don't tell me you're sure he's all right," she snapped. "You can't possibly be sure, so don't tell me that."

"All right," he whispered. "I won't."

Her expression softened. She gazed at the rugged topography of her husband's face, the features she knew so well. Ada had always been attractive in a sturdy, Amish way, a bit tomboyish with her prominent jaw and cropped hair, but Buddy was the striking one, the guy with movie star looks. Even after they were married, women flirted shamelessly. But he never strayed, not once, even after Ada turned fifty and added a few pounds to her solid frame. "I'm sorry, sweetheart," Ada sighed. "What were you going to say?"

"That I'm sure he's all right."

Twenty agonizing minutes later, Ada managed to get hold of her son. "He's fine!" she shouted.

"Told you," Buddy muttered.

When the tornado struck, Colin happened to be in Ponder, two towns north of Placid, at a sales meeting. The moment the news broke, he zoomed out of there, only to be pulled over and issued a speeding ticket. "Didn't you tell the policeman why you were rushing home?" Ada asked.

"It was a policewoman, and her radio was broken so she hadn't heard about the tornado yet." Colin continued detailing the daytime nightmare. When he arrived home, his home wasn't there. Neither were his wife or three daughters. Margaret, Tara, Olivia, and Vivien were entombed in the rubble of their flattened rustic-style house. The tornado gobbled the entire structure and then spit out the stone, wood, and bone it couldn't digest.

Ada was at a loss for words. Her alert mind never let her down, but this time it was faltering.

"That policewoman was pretty," Colin said. "Her red hair looked nice with the blue uniform."

"Oh Colin," she murmured. "Where are you now?"

"Standing where the living room used to be," he said, sounding lost and vulnerable. Ada recalled his sweet voice at age nine, calling from sleep-away camp, wanting to come home three weeks early.

"Don't go anywhere," she instructed. "Your father and I should be there in about fifteen minutes. You won't leave?"

"I won't leave," he responded slowly. "There's no place to go."

Ada clicked off, then delivered the news to Buddy.

"My God," Buddy whispered.

"His wife and daughters are gone and he's talking about the policewoman who gave him a ticket."

"He's in shock."

"Right."

"We need to be strong for him," Buddy stated. "You can't get all gooey and fall apart. If he hasn't fallen apart already, he *will*. We have to put him back together."

Ada nodded in agreement, suddenly aware she was wearing a mask of tears. Standing forlornly in the middle of the rubble, like a scarecrow, Colin Klock registered no emotion when he saw his parents pull up in their familiar truck. All the life had drained out of him. Ada and Buddy approached their son with love and alarm, eyes on the ground, careful to avoid stepping on broken glass, bricks, twigs, branches, pieces of terracotta pots, eating utensils, a two-slice toaster, and other debris. They gently embraced him. He returned the embrace with the energy of someone who'd just come out of surgery.

"Oh Colin," Ada murmured with deep sadness. "We're so sorry. We'll stay with you as long as you need."

"That's right," Buddy concurred. "We'll get you through this, son."

"I just finished re-doing the den," Colin said in a dull monotone. "I installed oak wall paneling." He kneeled down and picked up a splintered, foot-long piece of wood. "Do you like it?"

"I love the color," Ada remarked.

"Must've looked real nice on the wall," Buddy added.

"Let me see if I can find the new carpet," Colin said.

"No, that's all right," Ada insisted. "Save your strength, honey."

"Couldn't you afford a bigger toaster?" Buddy asked, looking at the ravaged one on the ground. "We would've bought one for you."

"We had a four-slice toaster," Colin said. "*That* one must've belonged to someone else." He paused. "My neighbor drove by, said people were gathering down by the docks. The ones who survived, that is."

"Then why don't we head over there?" Buddy suggested. Ada grabbed hold of Colin's hand and led him to the truck.

The area by the docks was grassy, with tall trees and a row of sailboats. A concrete path cut through the well-maintained lawn, and freshly painted green benches had dotted the area. But most of the boats had been shattered by the tornado, and the benches were completely gone.

The remaining populace roamed around aimlessly, looking as if they'd just been released from an internment camp. Disheveled clothing, windblown hair, skin bruised and cut, stunned expressions. Many were dealing with multiple bereavements as well as the loss of homes, cars, books, computers, stamp collections and expensive exercise equipment. Stray dogs trotted down the street, sniffing for food and searching for familiar faces.

A small group of men huddled in a powwow, discussing plans to build a large makeshift tent; two of them held sails salvaged from boats. A short, dark-eyed woman talked to herself in a loud voice as she strolled the circumference of the area. "Everything happens for a reason, so there was a good reason this happened. We'll find out soon enough. In the meantime, let's rejoice. Everyone, rejoice for our survival!"

Ada and Buddy sensed it was up to them to help these traumatized people. But for the moment, they dealt with immediate issues, distributing the snacks and bottles of water they'd packed. Of the two restaurants in town, only Sherman's Famous Hot Dog Shack was still standing, miraculously untouched by the tornado. Phyllis

Potter's Food Emporium had been decimated. The Popular Popsicle Shop, smashed completely. Other than the hot dog shack, the only stores that survived were The All-American Mattress Barn and Gigi's Cuts & Curls. Gigi Shinkle had already attached a hand-written sign to her window: *All are welcome to use salon's shower for five minutes. Men between the ages of eighteen and thirty get ten to fifteen.*

Pam Postlethwaite was sitting on a small patch of grass, her back straight and head bent as if in prayer, black hair splayed across her face. A young child, Jensen, was asleep in a cotton blanket in her lap. Ada approached gingerly, carrying a bottle of water and a sandwich. "Hello," she greeted with a soothing voice.

Pam looked up. Though she didn't crack a smile, she seemed to welcome the company. "Hi," she responded.

"You are a little angel, aren't you!" Ada chirped to the baby.

"He's just waking up."

"He does look sleepy. I thought you might want some water and a bite to eat."

"Oh thank you," Pam said, taking the food and drink. "That's very thoughtful."

"You're very welcome. Ada Klock here."

Pam appeared puzzled. "It can't possibly be eight o'clock. It's still light out."

"No, that's my name," Ada explained. "And my husband Buddy Klock is on his way over. We lost our daughter-in-law and three grandchildren in the tornado."

Pam conveyed her condolences. "Mother Nature whisked my husband Gil away in a matter of seconds. If he hadn't stopped to grab Annette, he'd still be alive."

"What kind of a net did he need in a tornado?" Ada asked.

"Annette was our kitten," Pam explained. "To tell you the truth, I didn't want that damn cat to begin with."

"Did Annette survive?" Ada asked.

"No, she's gone with the wind along with Gil," Pam muttered. "But that animal has eight other lives, and poor Gil used up his one and only."

"You have to be grateful for your own life," Ada instructed, "and for the life of that precious baby in your lap." Just then, Buddy appeared, and introductions were made. "Pam lost her husband in the tornado."

"I'm sorry to hear that," Buddy said, looking at her with attentive, caring eyes. "We're here to help in any way."

"If it wasn't for this little one, I wouldn't see any reason to go on," Pam confessed.

"That's how you feel *now*," Buddy told her, "but you won't feel that way forever."

"We'll see, I guess."

Dusk arrived with a wallop and a surprising chill. Buddy boldly walked into The All-American Mattress Barn where owner Edison Bunker was taking inventory. "Buddy Klock here," he said, thrusting his hand out to be shaken. "Glad your place is still standing."

"That makes two of us," Edison said.

"We've got a lot of people who'll be sleeping under the stars tonight," Buddy told him. "On the dirty ground, the pavement, damp sand. Think you could donate a few mattresses?"

"You live in Placid?" Edison asked.

"No, but my son Colin does."

"Colin Klock. Name sounds familiar. Is he all right?"

"He's alive," Buddy explained, "but his wife and daughters... three little girls...they didn't make it."

With the help of several strong, proud Placidians, three dozen latex foam mattresses were lugged outside and plunked on the ground.

"Maybe there was a reason that store was spared," Ada told Buddy as they climbed into their truck. She was glad she brought a heavy wool sweater for their now-forgotten trip to the Smoky Mountains. By nine o'clock, she and Buddy were snuggling in the back of their truck. "We have to *do* more," Ada quietly urged.

"Yep," Buddy agreed.

"It's a desperate situation."

"Desperate."

By eight thirty the following morning, a small crowd had gathered outside Sherman's Famous Hot Dog Shack. That's where the Klocks found their son, standing a good twenty feet away from the establishment. Not only were hot dogs on the house, so were plates of hotcakes with hot dog slices on the side. Ham and eggs were available at the reduced price of fifty cents.

Ada and Buddy had never seen their son so withdrawn. Soaked in sorrow, he was obviously traumatized, but some were traumatized more than others, and he was one of the worst. The woman who talked to herself was another; she was still babbling as she shuffled toward the hot dog shack. "Food has been granted to us. It's ours for the eating. Let's all sit at the communal table, masticate, ruminate, and nourish ourselves as a human family that consumes pig products."

In the distance, Pam and baby Jensen were approaching. When Ada saw them, she instantly rushed over. "Did you sleep on one of the mattresses?" she asked.

"We shared one with Libby Duffy."

"Goodness. Three to a mattress," Ada sighed, leading the young woman to Colin. "I want you to meet our son Colin. Colin, this is Pam and adorable Jensen." Just then, Jensen began crying, and Pam went into "Rock-a-bye Baby" mode.

"May I hold him?" Ada asked. "Some toddlers love my white hair."

Pam hesitated a moment before handing Jensen to Ada, but after ten seconds in the older woman's arms, the baby stopped crying.

"Amazing," Pam said.

"Buddy and I will take care of him for a while," Ada said. "Why don't you two have some breakfast?" Without waiting for an answer, she and Buddy wandered away, noticing that the sign was no longer in the window of Gigi's Cuts & Curls. In its place, a small one read *Shower Shut Down*.

Pam and Colin ate their hotcakes and hot dog slices in silence while Ada and Buddy brainstormed nonstop. Ideas flowed. Concepts were conceptualized. An hour later, they returned to Sherman's Famous Hot Dog Shack with a contented Jensen.

By the end of the very long day, the mayor still hadn't arrived, but hundreds of food packets were distributed by volunteers from neighboring towns of Antique, Ponder, Smelt, Umbrage, and Mary Queen of Scots. News of the tornado was spreading across the country, and within a week, more than a ton of relief supplies had arrived at King Russet Municipal Airport.

"Will you trust us?" Buddy asked Pam and Colin as the sun was setting on the fifth day.

"Trust you about what?" Colin inquired. He was accustomed to the sometimes radical ideas of his parents.

"We're going to ask you to do something," Buddy said, "and we want your cooperation." Buddy and Ada sent each other a glance.

"What do you want us to do?" Colin asked.

"Get married. To each other."

Colin and Pam froze. "Pam and this precious baby need a husband and a father," Ada explained, lovingly stroking a curl of hair out of Jensen's eyes.

"And Colin, there's nothing you need more than a new family to care for," Buddy instructed. The message hovered in the air with no fanfare, no bells ringing or balloons rising. The concept had nothing to do with grand passion or everlasting love. Two separate individuals shattered by circumstances would merge lives in order to survive with the most possible ease. It was that simple.

Pam and Colin covertly appraised one another as Ada spoke. "You're in the midst of an emotional trauma, so you're not capable of thinking rationally."

"Right," Buddy agreed. "As your parents, we decided to think *for* you."

"Is this OK with you, honey?" Ada asked Pam. "This union?"

Pam turned to Colin. "You're not a cat person, are you?" she asked.

"No."

"Then I'm good," she replied nonchalantly, as if purchasing a new frying pan. "Colin?" Buddy asked.

"We insist, honey," Ada stated.

"Then sure, why not?"

Luckily, the minister had survived the natural disaster and agreed to marry the young couple. After the official ceremony took place on the devastated lot where the old church used to stand, Ada and Buddy played with the baby while the newlyweds enjoyed a one-hour honeymoon behind what was left of the Placid Cheese Pavilion. Pam emerged with a delirious smile on her face, and Colin moved with an exuberant bounce in his step.

This was the first of several marriages arranged by the Klocks. Working on instinct alone, they matched men and women who seemed suited to each other. They even matched one woman with another woman. Some of Placid's more conservative citizens were outraged by the entire enterprise. "On behalf of my wife's memory, I'm highly disgusted and horrified," shouted former town dentist Wally Frimmer. "It's one thing to set strangers up on a date, but to bring them together in the sacred bond of matrimony? That takes a lot of gall."

"We're sorry for your loss," Buddy said, "but we're also sorry you feel this way."

"I think you're cuckoo," he responded. "And that makes you damn cuckoo Klocks."

"Look at the state you're in," Ada said. "Eyes red, spirit dead, making tired puns. Probably constipated from all those hot dogs. Do you think your late wife would want you to spend your life this way? Wouldn't she prefer to see you move forward productively, surrounded by a supportive new family?"

"Not if it was arranged by Dolly Levi."

As more time passed, the skeptics who initially rallied against the idea came around; their daily needs began to eclipse their long-held ideals about love and marriage. Perfection was no longer the goal. Simply making it through the day was lofty enough.

Ada and Buddy Klock felt their mission was complete. They climbed into their clattering old pickup truck and headed home, smiles sewn on their mature, satisfied faces. They would make new arrangements for their trip to the Smoky Mountains.

(Note: In the aftermath of the earthquake that devastated Sichuan province, China, and killed 87,000 people in 2008, thousands of "earthquakes marriages" were arranged in an attempt to urge grief-stricken survivors to move forward.)

The Charismatic Accountant

Allan Barnicle could hardly believe it. For the first time in the show's extraordinary history, a certified public accountant was asked to host Saturday Night Live.

Allan had never acted on stage or performed in a comedy club, never dreamed of a career in front of the camera; he didn't even consider himself particularly funny. But thanks to a winning personality and an infectious smile, plus the insistence of fellow accountant Gordon Funderburk, Allan was the lucky guy, the carefully chosen amateur.

The American public had become tired of talentless, emaciated celebutantes and obnoxious reality TV stars. Organizations began to boycott US Weekly and picket the offices of People. Tabloids folded. Audiences were fed up with disgraced politicians trying to redeem their reputations on chat shows on the advice of savvy public relations consultants. The networks buckled under the pressure and were forced to produce thoughtful, intelligent dramatic shows as well as sitcoms that were actually funny. The message was clear: the public wanted actors to act, not to create fragrances or share diet tips or write lame tell-all books.

Executive producer Lorne Michaels decided to take part in the anti-celebrity movement with an episode of Saturday Night Live. NBC talent scouts scoured the tri-state area in search of a funny, charismatic unknown. Gordon, a geeky, prematurely gray Princeton grad who worked closely with Allan at the office, had heard about the search and encouraged Allan to audition. "But I have no experience," he groused.

"That's what they're looking for – people with no experience."

"Why don't you try out?" Allan asked.

"Who do you think people would rather watch – a skinny nerd with acne or a well-built babe magnet with boyish good looks?"

"You're not that skinny," Allan said.

The audition couldn't have gone any better, and the search was narrowed down to three guys and a gal.

While sitting in the reception area of NBC's midtown office, Allan and the solitary female struck up a conversation. "I'm Amanda Vreeland," the vivacious redhead said. "No relation to Diana."

"I didn't think women were named Amanda except in soap operas," Allan joked, desperately trying to place the name Diana Vreeland.

A smile lit up Amanda's flawless, slightly freckled face. With her thick-rimmed glasses, she was the type featured in men's magazines: the prudish brainiac who whips off her glasses, rips off her blouse and becomes a veritable hottie. "What do you do?" she asked.

"Accountant. You?"

"I work with the mentally ill," she replied. "People with schizophrenia or schizoaffective disorder. Some of my clients also suffer from Axis II personality disorders like borderline, histrionic, or obsessive-compulsive behavior."

"That's cool." The response followed an awkward pause.

"Why is that cool?" she inquired.

"Because compared to them, I'll be a snap to deal with."

Amanda didn't appreciate jokes about her profession, but she knew Allan meant no harm, and she could hardly wait to crawl into his bed and make him beg. Little gave her more pleasure than watching a confident, cocksure man beg for mercy.

"Sorry," Allan apologized with shame. "What I just told you was in extremely bad taste."

"Yes, it was."

"Now that I'm being considered for Saturday Night Live, I try to be funny all the time. Sometimes it backfires."

"Well," she chuckled, "you can make it up to me tonight."

Again Allan paused, this time without the awkwardness. "Did I hear that right?" he asked, wondering if Amanda was some kind of plant, and this was all part of his audition.

"Sure did."

After a French-Asian fusion dinner and the best chocolate souffle either of them had ever tasted, the couple strolled toward Amanda's place. The bright full moon illuminated the jam-parked cars and well-dressed pedestrians on Gramercy Park Street. A uniformed doorman welcomed them to the building. Sexual tension filled the elevator. The moment they walked through the door of the apartment, Amanda ripped open his shirt, removed his pants, and handcuffed Allan to a leg of her dark oak dining room table. In the dim light of a lavender-scented candle, she massaged his body and struck his buttocks with a tennis racket until he begged for mercy. Then they retreated to her bedroom, tennis racket in tow, and didn't emerge for several hours.

The following Wednesday morning, Allan got word that he'd been chosen as host for the November 3rd edition of Saturday Night Live. He immediately shared the news with Gordon. "Congratulations!" Gordon beamed. "I knew you could do it."

"I owe it all to you, man!" .

"You're going to be a household name in houses other than yours, mine and your mother's," Gordon excitedly said. "This is so great."

"I'm taking you to lunch, my friend," Allan insisted.

"It's barely eleven o'clock."

"We'll eat light."

Over a pepperoni pizza with spinach, mushrooms and extra garlic, the guys discussed Allan's great fortune and Gordon's grand failure in their search for the right woman. "I've been cursed," Gordon admitted. "My first exploit didn't occur till a year after college, and it was pretty dismal." He reached for his second slice of pizza. "When was yours?"

"A week before high school," Allan said. "It was fantastic."

"People need to be touched. Going years without physical contact can drive a man mad, you know."

"That's why you have to be with the wrong woman until you meet the right one," Allan explained. "In fact, you have to be with a lot of wrong ones. Why don't you ask Nanette out?" It was common knowledge that Gordon was crazy about Nanette Krupp, a rail-thin, perky blonde colleague with a bold sense of style.

"I don't think she's into me," Gordon replied with regret.

"You won't know for sure until you ask," Allan said through a mouthful of mushrooms. "Just take the plunge, bro."

Nanette got wind of Allan's big news at three in the afternoon, and she breezed down the hall in a black leather mini dress with studs on the shoulder pads. "You sly, talented cookie!" she gushed, throwing her bare arms around Allan's torso and keeping them there longer than he would've liked. "I knew you had splendid business acumen but who knew you had a sense of humor?" Just then, Gordon knocked twice and nervously stepped into the office.

"Did you hear about Saturday Night Live?" Nanette asked.

"Yes," Gordon said. "Amazing. And your dress is beyond amazing."

"Thanks," she chirped. "Diana Vreeland once said Never fear being vulgar, just boring."

"Diana Vreeland," Allan mumbled.

"Vogue's greatest editor."

"Of course," he said, nodded. "Did you know it was Gordon's idea that I try out for the show? If it wasn't for him, none of this would've happened."

"Good going, Gordon," Nanette said without looking at him.

"Listen, I decided to throw a viewing party," Gordon announced. "I'll invite the whole gang. Just had the carpet shampooed." He gazed at Nanette longingly.

She turned to Allan. "Will you come?" she asked with excitement in her eyes.

"Not sure how late I'll be, but I'll definitely go," he said.

"I hope you can come over right after the taping," Nanette pouted. "We'll all want to hug our new star."

"Until I get there, you'll have this guy to hug. He's a great hugger and he knows how to throw a blowout bash," Allan said, eyes on Gordon. "Time to get back to work, kids. Client meeting at four."

"Sure thing." Gordon ran to the door and opened it for his unrequited love. Nanette followed, shooting Allan a quick glance over her shoulder before disappearing into the hallway.

Thrilled to have her all to himself, if only for a few fleeting seconds, Gordon asked his great love the first question that popped into his head. "Are you an only child?"

"Middle," she chirped. "Smack in the middle of prepping a profit and loss statement. By the way, you reek of garlic, Gordon." With that, she headed out, leaving him behind like a dead squirrel on the side of the road.

That evening, Allan and Amanda celebrated the phenomenal

news with a delicious Thai dinner, after which they headed back to Amanda's place where once again she handcuffed him to her dining room table. "Tell me you're sorry you got the SNL gig instead of me," she crowed with subversive glee.

"I'm sorry," he moaned with a combination of titillation and trepidation.

"Just how sorry?" she asked.

"Very, very. I'm the sorriest guy on the planet."

"Don't you think you deserve a beating for being such a bad boy?"

"Yes I do," he told her. "Absolutely." After a pause: "But not too hard."

Instead of grabbing her tennis racket, she marched to the bookshelf and snatched a hardcover copy of Naked Lunch. The book felt as heavy as a brick.

The week before the Saturday Night Live broadcast was one of the most grueling of Allan's life. There were pitch meetings, read-throughs, rehearsals. Sketches were written, rewritten and rewritten again, rehearsed and re-rehearsed. On Friday, costume fittings took time away from rehearsing. On the day of the taping, rehearsals continued until a full dress rehearsal in front of a studio audience. Allan relished every second of this once-in-a-lifetime experience.

In the first sketch, Allan would play a certified public accountant dealing with a client from hell. Another sketch would require him to don a wavy, shoulder-length blond wig and act the part of a demanding, self-absorbed rock star. In another, he would play a conservative suburban dad whose teenage daughter was arrested for indecent exposure at a shopping mall. The musical guest would be Felicia Laufer, a professor of medieval history at Hunter College.

On the big night, Amanda sat next to Allan's proud parents Irene and Jim. They made the journey from Clifton, New Jersey to be part of the studio audience despite Irene's active gallstones.

An hour before the show began, Allan called Gordon on his cell. "I want this night to be great for both of us," he said.

"Me, too," Gordon told him. "I'm pulling for you."

"And I'm pulling for you. If things aren't going well with Nanette, remind her that it was your idea for me to audition for the show."

"I'll do that. Now go out there and be your best."

"I'll try," Allan said.

An enthusiastic group of twenty colleagues showed up at Gordon's downtown apartment with its beige carpet, beige curtains, moldy bathroom, and kitchen cabinets in need of remodeling. Several disturbing Diane Arbus black-and-white prints on the walls gave the place an eerie, macabre vibe. A half circle of chairs was set up in front of the flat-screen TV.

The last to arrive, Nanette appeared in a bright yellow halter dress with rhinestone-studded stilettos and spiked hair. The sight of her standing in the doorway heated Gordon with a rush of desire. Everyone else became irrelevant. "You look beyond beautiful," he told her.

"Yellow's a good color for me," she explained as she stepped into the apartment. "Blue is your color."

"I'm wearing brown," Gordon said.

"I know. But blue is your color."

"Oh. I'll remember that," he replied, "How about a drink?"

"Sure. Circus Rickey," she said, her eyes circling the room to see who was there.

"I'm not familiar with that," Gordon said apologetically.

"Then anything with gin will do."

"Got it. There's catered food on the dining room table."

Nanette kicked off her stilettos and stretched out on the recently shampooed carpet. "I'm wearing yellow because it's supposed to be good for the gallbladder," she told her colleague Abe.

"You think your gallbladder gives a shit what color you have on?" he asked with a laugh.

"You need to be more attuned, Abey baby. Attune yourself, and buy some decent clothes. I guarantee you'd get laid more."

When Don Pardo announced, "And your host, Allan Barnicle," the crowd at Gordon's place erupted in ecstatic whoops and hollers.

Allan made his way to the middle of the stage. When the applause died down, he said, "In case you're wondering who I am, I was recently made partner in the accounting firm of Preston Choi Cornleaf Halberstadt Sanz Newkirk Barnicle & Briggs." The studio audience broke into laughter. "That wasn't supposed to be funny," he added with a sheepish grin.

Allan came across as a natural, likeable host. "We've got a great show for you," he said. "Felicia Laufer is here." The studio audience applauded politely, not knowing who Felicia Laufer was. Then the TV screen dipped to black.

A second later, the first sketch began. It was obvious Allan was reading cue cards. He came across as stiff and uncomfortable.

In the second sketch, Allan was a walking sight gag in a long blond wig and glittering gold jacket. But when it came time to speak, he was awkward and not the least bit funny. He just couldn't deliver dialogue. After the commercial break, Allan introduced musical guest Felicia Laufer who possessed the lung-busting, headache-inducing vocal power of Celine Dion.

During the musical performance, Nanette struggled up from the carpet and made her way to the bathroom to relieve her bursting bladder and see if her host had anything interesting in his medicine cabinet. Gordon took this opportunity to covertly kick one of her stilettos into the living room closet. After Felicia Laufer's song, several guests asked for Tylenol.

In the next sketch, Allan played the harried suburban dad. This time, he was so afraid he'd make a fool of himself that he could barely speak. He looked frightened, alarmed, like a burglar knowing the police were about to break in.

At Gordon's place, half-filled wine glasses froze in midair. "This can't be for real," Abe said.

"No, no," Nanette shook her head. "Poor Allan. This is so embarrassing."

The show's regulars rushed to Allan's defense, but the sketch was agony for the studio audience and TV viewers alike.

Seated in a chintz armchair, Gordon seemed to be in another world, staring at something beyond the flat screen TV. "Maybe I should've auditioned," he mumbled.

Allan's abysmal performance dampened the evening for everyone at Gordon's gathering. By the end of the show, nobody could crack a smile. This was not the way the host had intended the evening to end. He'd hoped the clinking of ice cubes and sound of laughter would continue until the wee hours. He'd thought Allan might make a surprise appearance. He had even dared to imagine Nanette spending the night and sampling his pumpkin pancakes the following morning, unless she preferred Raisin Bran or Honey Bunches of Oats.

Guests began to leave in clusters of two and three. "Has anybody seen my red shoe?" Nanette called out, searching under the sofa. No one had seen it. Five minutes later, Nanette was the only remaining guest. "Where the fuck could it be, Gordon?"

"Let's look in the bedroom."

"I didn't set foot in the bedroom," she responded.

"Maybe someone kicked it in there by accident."

A bizarre black and white print hung on the wall above Gordon's dresser. "What is that monstrosity?" Nanette asked.

"It's a Diane Arbus photograph called Screaming Woman With Blood On Her Hands."

"And you hung it on your bedroom wall because...?"

"It's high art," he explained.

"Oh, I see. You have to be high to appreciate it." Just then, Gordon's lips lunged for Nanette's throat. "What are you doing?" she yelled.

"Trying to kiss the neck of a swan," he said.

"Go to the Bronx Zoo! Get the hell away from me!"

With manic force, Gordon pushed her onto the platform bed. Then, as he hoisted himself up onto the extra firm mattress, Nanette lifted her legs and kicked him powerfully in the femur with her remaining stiletto. He screamed in pain, plunging backwards onto the hardwood floor.

Nanette instantly jumped off the bed. "You fucking rodent!" she shrieked. "If you ever talk to me, touch me, or even look at me at the office again, I'll report you to Human Resources, the entire board of directors, and the police."

"I'm the one who encouraged Allan to audition for Saturday Night Live," Gordon whimpered from the floor.

"Yeah, and that alone proves your stupidity." Nanette raced out of the apartment, still down a stiletto.

Gordon remained supine for several minutes. "I told you, Allan," he moaned, struggling to stand up. "I don't think she's into me."

A half hour later, the humiliated SNL host arrived at Gordon's doorstep looking haggard and despondent. "I sure hope your night went better than mine," Allan said. "Did everybody go home?"

"Yeah," Gordon reported. "Nanette was the last to leave."

"That's a good sign," Allan said with encouragement.

"Not really. She threatened to call the cops if I ever looked at her again."

"Gordon, bro, that's not a good sign."

"I didn't think so either." He shook his head forlornly.

Allan plopped down on the sofa and shut his eyes. "Hey, can I hide out here for a day or two?" he asked. "I don't think I can face the world for a while."

"Stay as long as you want," Gordon replied. "I can't face the world either, not until I come to grips with the fact that I'll be alone for the rest of my rotten life."

"She's just one chick. There are plenty of others in the coop." Allan opened his tired eyes and scanned the room. "Look at all that booze and wine. Nobody touched it."

"We didn't feel like celebrating," Gordon explained.

"How about you and I start right now and we won't stop till half those bottles are empty?" Allan proposed.

Gordon bolted up with a surge of energy. "That's the best idea I've heard since…well, since I don't know when."

"Since you suggested I audition for Saturday Night Live?" Allan asked. "Since I agreed to do something I was completely, ridiculously unqualified for?"

Gordon did something he hadn't expected to do for several months. He laughed out loud. So did Allan.

The Birth of Roget's Thesaurus

(This story contains 1% fact.)

IT TOOK BRITISH SURGEON AND INVENTOR PM Roget 47 years to create the thesaurus. This was the esteemed doctor's lifelong obsession. He lived and breathed synonyms. An audiotape of Roget's inaugural creative session was recently discovered at the British Library. According to Senior Manager Abigail Cosgrove-Cumberbatch, the discovery was nothing short of miraculous. "The tape was gathering dust for a half century," Cosgrove-Cumberbatch reports. "If I hadn't assigned my assistant to take inventory, we still wouldn't know about its existence, and what a loss that would be."

Cosgrove-Cumberbatch is an avid activist for the English language. "At the end of the day, all we have is the spoken word," she explains with passion. "We may lose our homes, our husbands and our dignity, our children may refuse to take our calls, but we still hold onto our language." *Holding onto Our Language*, Cosgrove-Cumberbatch's very first book, will be published by Bennett, Rue & Thames. According to a press release, the tome will be released "when we find the perfect place for vernacular titles appropriate for the reading public."

Assisted by PM Roget's wife Nan, who took dictation in longhand, the audiotape documents the birth of this vital reference book. The following is a transcript:

```
PM:   We should start, of course, with A.
NAN:  Not necessarily.
PM:   Why not?
NAN: Let's be bold and jump ahead to L in honor
of ourprecious Lilly. We'll get to A later.
PM:   All right then. L-A-A. Nothing.
NAN:  L-A-B. Lab.
PM:  Lab is short for laboratory. Not a word
unto itself. Moving on. L-A-B-A. Nothing.
NAN:  L-A-B-O-R. Labor.
PM:   Yes, labor. Noun. Activity. Endeavor.
NAN:  Good.
PM:   Industry.
NAN:  Industry is not a synonym for labor.
PM:   It can be used as a synonym.
NAN:  Not to my thinking.
PM:   I didn't ask for your thinking, only for
your writing. Ijust realized something:  Label
should come beforelabor.
NAN:  Of course. Label is a…trademark, design.
PM:  Also epithet, classification.
NAN:  Classification?  I think not.
PM:   I don't think not.
NAN:  Just because I classify you as stubborn
doesn't meanI'm assigning a label.
PM:   Write it down.
NAN:  I'm bored with L. Let's go to D for our
darlingDebbie.
PM:   For Debbie. D-A-A. Nothing. D-A-B. Dab.
Verb. To smear.
NAN:  To touch.
```

```
PM:    No. I can touch you without dabbing you.
Dabbingimplies something on your fingertips
like a stingingointment or a poisonous liquid
that I might smearon your tongue while you're
asleep.
NAN:   I see.
PM:    Let's jump ahead to W in honor of our
frightfulWinifred.
NAN:   Fine.
PM:    Werewolf. A predatory mammal that sucks
the bloodfrom its prey. You must have scores of
synonymsfor that.
NAN:   No, darling. Waste and want and weakling
wouldprecede werewolf, wouldn't they?
PM:   They would. So would wallop. Verb. To bash,
belt,pummel, slug in the jaw with unrestrained
force.
```

At this point, the audiotape goes silent for fifteen seconds. Then comes the rustling of paper and the deep voice of Dr. Roget.

```
PM:    I will begin with the letter A. A-L-O-N-E.
Alone. Adjective. Solo. Single. Unaccompanied.
Ecstaticbeyond measure.
```

The recording continues for several hours without the assistance of Nan.

"The tape is music to my ears," says Cosgrove-Cumberbatch. "Imagine a Shakespearean scholar coming upon an undiscovered work by the Bard. That's how thrilling this is." When asked about the contentious bickering of the Rogets, she responds, "When creative juices are flowing, friction is often a natural part of the process." The marriage of the Rogets was shaky at best, but according to published reports, the couple remained together for the sake of the thesaurus.

"Humiliation goes with the territory," Cosgrove-Cumberbatch added. "Now let me take this opportunity to dispel rumors about Roget's purported erectile dysfunction. They are categorically false." Some experts believe Algerian philosopher Albert Camus was the culprit, spreading the rumors, deliberately trying to defile the reputation of Dr. Roget out of envy. "You know what they say: Hell hath no fury like a jealous Algerian."

The tape has been placed in the British Library which also houses the 1902 recording of Sarah Bernhardt 's "Phaedre," a self-portrait of Sir George Gardiner (considered the ugliest member of Parliament in British history), and the 1996 hit single "Wannabe" by the Spice Girls.

The facts:.

- PM Roget created the thesaurus.

Last Hope in Chagrin Falls

TAMMY HICKS, the most humble, well-liked hairdresser in the small town of Tendency, Idaho, decided to throw a huge bake sale to raise money for her upcoming electroconvulsive therapy.

Tammy's best friend, Mona Razzle, owned Yeast Perfection, the largest bakery in all of Watercress County. She promised to donate apple dapple bundt cakes, fan tan rolls, and a truckload of peach and blueberry cobblers.

Mona convinced her commitment-phobic boyfriend, Keith, to commit to providing currant scones. Red currant scones and black currant scones were the big sellers at Keith's popular bake shop, Dough Rising. Breezy Lefebvre, a bubbly forty-year-old with a French accent many suspected was phony as plastic fruit, volunteered her baguettes, orange tartletts and famous yellow sponge cake soaked in Grand Marnier. Breezy's patisserie, Baking Love, had just celebrated its fifth anniversary.

The one other bakery in town, I. M. Pie, was run by a Dutch ex-beauty queen named Ilke Mae Smit. From afar, I.M. (as her friends called her) seemed an ethereal wonder, a slice of pure seductiveness, but upon closer inspection a certain toughness revealed itself, suggesting

Ilke Mae had survived her share of struggle. It was rumored that she took her ample winnings from a pageant in Amsterdam and fled to America, leaving her starving mother on the streets of Zaltbommel without so much as a guilder.

"Are you sure you don't want to ask Ilke Mae to pitch in?" Mona inquired one boring, wet Monday as Tammy helped her open shop. "People love those cakes of hers."

"We don't need the baked goods of a bad person," Tammy grunted as she lifted a box full of fondant. The sound of distant thunder interrupted the tranquility of the morning.

Soft-spoken, tenderhearted Tammy had suffered severe mood swings since the age of eleven. She'd spent hours, sometimes days, in her gloomy room, petrified that if she climbed out of bed she'd fall into an abyss, like an elevator with cut cables. She idealized death and contemplated suicide, and once spent an entire weekend cleaning out her closet so that her mother wouldn't have too many items to sort through when she was gone.

Clearly, the crash made matters worse. Tammy's parents and younger brother were killed in a brutal car accident on the drive home from a new Szechuan restaurant (Ten Yen) that was garnering raves around town. Sixteen at the time, Tammy had been too despondent to go along (but had asked them to bring her an order of Twice Cooked Pork). This tragic, immutable event arrived with more than a little irony: The one who obsessed about death became the last living member of her immediate family.

Soon the orphaned girl's two young cousins perished under rather peculiar circumstances, leaving Aunt Jinx as Tammy's only living relative - not that she played an active part in Tammy's life. In fact, she only saw the teenage girl a few times a year, usually during holidays when Jinx's home was crowded with dozens of wealthy, well-dressed neighbors. Tammy felt entirely out of place at these festivities, but she attended in order to spend what little face-time her aunt gave her.

It was Dr. Kurt von Zeubriggon who finally diagnosed Tammy with Stage 2 bipolar disorder. Over a period of years, the incredibly patient patient took one antidepressant after the next, sometimes combining two or three or four, adding atypical antipsychotics to the mix. Nothing worked. The feelings of panic, hopelessness and despair didn't diminish. After the frustrating trial and error (which turned out to be all error), Dr. von Zeubriggon sent Tammy to Dr. Kylah Watts, a specialist in electroconvulsive therapy in the progressive town of Chagrin Falls, fifty miles east.

A petite woman with imperfect skin and straight grayish hair that was perpetually damp, Dr. Watts resembled a dry roasted peanut. She expertly provided Tammy with the pertinent information about electroconvulsive therapy, ECT for short.

At the conclusion of their first meeting, Tammy decided to take the plunge. "I'll sign up for the whole package," she announced, as if making the decision to spend two weeks at a luxury hotel in Honolulu. The only stumbling block was the cost. Medical insurance would only cover a fraction of it, and Tammy realized the final figure could be in the tens of thousands. Somehow, she sensed, she would raise the money. Somehow, she felt, her Aunt Jinx would play a pivotal role in this arduous process.

"Sit!" Aunt Jinx barked like a tough-as-nails dog trainer. "Try a dark raspberry truffle. They're Swiss."

Tammy nervously climbed onto an elegant chair that had been shipped from Versailles, so Jinx once said. The entire estate of Jinx Pontius was a wealthy widow's paradise. "I love truffles," Tammy murmured, knowing anything she uttered would go in one of her aunt's ears and out the other. She wondered if she should even bother to tell Jinx that her bouffant jet black hair looked like tail fins on a vintage Cadillac.

"To what do I owe this visit?" Jinx always got straight down to business.

"Well," Tammy began, clumsily shifting on the velvet cushion, "I'm having a bake sale three weeks from Sunday."

"How nice," Jinx piped. "Count me in for a seedless rye."

"Oh. Sure. Thanks. But the purpose of the event is to raise money for a medical procedure I need called electroconvulsive therapy, or ECT. All the bakers in town have agreed to donate pies and cakes, and sell them for fifty or a hundred dollars."

"I see," Jinx stuffed a truffle in her mouth.

"The treatment is performed at the hospital in Chagrin Falls. They don't do it anywhere in Watercress, Shirley, or Daylight Counties."

"Nobody does it in Daylight?" she asked.

"No." Tammy wished she would stop interrupting. "The reason I'm here is that I need a place to hold this bake sale, and I thought your beautiful back yard would be ideal."

"*My* back yard?" Jinx screeched, eyeballs popping out of their sockets. "My back *yard*?"

"Yes, your big yard... in the back."

"It's simply out of the question."

"Why is that?" Tammy asked.

"Because I'm too busy with my civic duties this month."

"Aunt Jinx, I've never asked you for a favor."

"That's why we're so close."

"But I'm asking *now*," Tammy begged. "It's only one afternoon, and we'll direct everybody straight to the back. That way, no one has to set foot in your exquisite house."

"To raise money so you can zap electricity into your brain?" Jinx asked with a chuckle. "It's too jolting to think about."

"Nothing else has worked. This is my last resort."

"I believe you can do anything if you set your mind to it," she declared.

"This is what I want to do," Tammy replied with surprising force. "This is what I've set my mind to." Then came a pause so pregnant that Jinx knew something was on its way, traveling rapidly down the canal, seconds away from arrival. "You must miss your girls," Tammy said.

No one in Tendency suspected Jinx of playing any part in the deaths of her daughters Amelia and Cecelia. Each was ruled accidental, despite the fact that both took their own lives. "Why are you bringing my daughters up?" Jinx hissed.

"Because I miss them a lot," Tammy replied calmly. "We grew up together."

"Well, they're gone."

"They're gone because they couldn't bear their overbearing mother," Tammy stated in a straightforward manner. "That's why they ended it. I have letters from Amelia."

"Her death was not deliberate!" Jinx shouted.

"Oh, did the noose accidentally find its way around her neck?" Tammy asked. "And who wrote that suicide note, Anne Sexton?"

"What are you implying, young lady?" Jinx hissed.

"I don't think you'd want the people of Tendency to know the truth about your daughters, would you? Or maybe I'm wrong. Maybe you *wouldn't* mind."

Jinx had never seen Tammy so manipulative; she couldn't help feeling a small amount of pride. Despite her ardent protest, the notion of this bake sale actually appealed to Jinx; playing hostess to the residents of Tendency would only enhance her standing in the community. "I don't want to see a single crumb afterwards," Jinx warned.

"You won't!" Tammy shouted victoriously. "Thank you, Aunt Jinx, thank you so much."

The weather on Tammy's big day was deliciously cool. Despite a prediction of clear skies, a gray cloud hung ominously in the distance. Twenty large tables were set up in the beautiful, spacious back yard of Jinx's estate. Mona manned the cheesecake and cobblers. Keith stood behind his scones as well as two dozen of his popular glazed dunking sticks. Breezy Lefebvre offered her baguettes, orange tartletts and brioche, calling everyone "cherie." Several bakers from neighboring towns also agreed to take part, arriving with big boxes of their specialties.

At exactly noon, community members began to wander in. Whether it was the smell of fresh bread wafting through the air or the deep concern everyone had for Tammy and her plight, several hundred carb-loving souls milled about, grabbing their wallets and opening their fanny packs, handing over cold, hard cash in exchange for warm, soft Bundt cakes and cobblers.

At first, Tammy thought she spotted a mirage – a statuesque vision carrying two shopping bags as if they were heavy suitcases, heading to a train station. As the figure came closer, Tammy recognized Ilke Mae Smit, looking like she just awakened from a sensual sleep. "Hello Tammy," Ilke Mae said in a soft, subdued tone, "I thought you could use some of my Dutch apple pies, banana nut muffins, and lemon cakes with royal white frosting."

Deeply touched, Tammy led the Dutch goddess to an empty spot. Not only did Ilke Mae provide her much loved pies, muffins and cakes, she brought two dozen cookies in the shape of stars and planets.

Jinx waited until two o'clock to make her grand entrance.

Imperiously, she waved to the crowd, then strolled the grounds like a queen among her subjects, sampling a danish here, some corn bread there. When she took a bite of the peach cobbler, she experienced a profound sensual pleasure the likes of which she hadn't encountered in decades. "Even the birds above us are happy," she said, gazing at a flock flying in a V-shaped formation.

Twenty minutes after Jinx's appearance, the soothing calm of the event was rocked by the sound of thunder. The ominous cloud, hanging directly over the back yard, had expanded and darkened the sky. "It's a shroud," Tammy whispered to Mona, "ready to blanket the town." Not ten seconds later, rain came pouring down, slamming the tables like nails being hammered into wood. This was no light rainstorm; it was one of the most powerful showers Tendency had ever seen. Pandemonium ensued as people ran in all directions, many of them shielding their small children and just-purchased breads and cakes with fur-lined coats and jackets.

Luckily, the overwhelming majority of baked goods had been sold before the weather changed and the chaos began, and enough money had been raised.

Tammy's first treatment was scheduled for the second Monday of June. She was instructed by Dr. Watts to avoid eating after ten o'clock the previous night.

Mona drove her hungry, jittery friend to the towering hospital in Chagrin Falls. The procedure was to begin at ten o'clock sharp and would take less than an hour.

The women arrived early, so they sat silently in the waiting room, too tense to read any of the magazines strewn across the coffee table. Dr. Watts appeared. Mona gave Tammy a hug, then the diminutive doctor escorted Tammy to the treatment room.

There was a set of twin beds, several medical machines, and a no-nonsense nurse busy with last minute preparations. It didn't look at all like science fiction, the way Tammy had imagined, and she wasn't sure if she was relieved or disappointed.

After changing into the thin, blue hospital gown, Tammy climbed onto the bed closest to the machines. Dr. Watts introduced her to Dr. Underwood, the anesthesiologist. "I'll be putting you to sleep," he announced with a warm smile.

Twenty minutes later, the procedure was complete. When Tammy woke up, her head was pounding. Helena handed her a mild painkiller and a paper cup filled with water. "If you don't feel better in a few hours, please call us and the doctor will prescribe something stronger," she advised.

Every few minutes on the long drive home, Mona asked Tammy if she felt any different. The answer was the same each time: Tammy didn't feel any better and she didn't feel any worse.

Two days later, Tammy's second treatment took place. Two days after that, the third treatment was administered.

One day after Tammy's eighth treatment, she was picking up a few items at the grocery store. Everything seemed easier than usual – breathing, walking, thinking. She resorted to logic to find the source of her newfound contentment, asking herself if anything had changed either socially or at the salon. The answer was no. Then she wondered if her mind was playing a trick on her. She'd become so accustomed to undergoing ECT with no result that she honestly didn't connect her feeling of lightness and pleasure with the medical procedure.

Suddenly Tammy froze. Could it be that the therapy kicked in? She thought. My God, is this what normal people feel like every day?

She realized this was how everything in her life had happened – oddly, unexpectedly, obliquely. Tammy wanted to jump on a trampoline and share her news with every person on the street. Instead, she found her way to a nearby bench where, in a flood of excitement, she crossed her legs and grinned from ear to ear, her sense of elation barely contained.

The Bludgeoning of a Burgeoning Young Artist

Freddy Hodge had always been ahead of his time. The visionary painter was born two weeks premature, kicking his way down the birth canal. The crib hadn't even been delivered, so the four-pound infant was forced to sleep between his parents on a tattered bed for the first few nights of his life.

At the age of seven, Freddy broke the nose of a boy who bullied the class nerd.

By the time he was twelve, Freddy had spent a night in jail for assault and battery after striking a bearded stranger who tried to feel his mother up on a train.

At fifteen, the rebellious boy was convicted of knocking out a store clerk and stealing art supplies. Tried as a minor, he was sentenced to ten days behind bars, plus probation.

The volatile teenager was plagued with anger issues, the bulk of his rage directed at his father, who deserted the family shortly after the boy's sixth birthday. The small remainder of Freddy's resentment was saved for his mother, who had turned their tranquil home into a hangout for bikers, hookers, and junkies drawn to the tattoo parlor in the living room.

Specializing in skull and snake tattoos, Wanda's artistic talent brought her celebrity status in the small town of Kennel, twenty miles from the Atlantic coast. Money flowed into Wanda's tattoo parlor, and most of it was spent on the purchase of ink, needles and cocaine.

At fourteen, Freddy begrudgingly learned the family trade. Irrefutably hot at sixteen, the girls in the neighborhood began throwing themselves at him (along with some of their mothers). Freddy found one of his passions: sex. Every other night he brought a new girl to the rickety bungalow he called home. Around the same time, Freddy discovered his other obsession: painting.

Just prior to turning twenty, Freddy was discovered by the renowned patron of the arts, Athena Easterling.

It was Athena's *modus operandi* to invite a new protégé into her estate every six months. Her most recent discovery, Dalton Rhys-Malone, a square-jawed painter whose work depicted sensual encounters in dimly lit breweries, was the first artist-in-residence who refused to walk away quietly. "You think you can snap your fingers and make me vanish?" he roared, glaring at his statuesque mentor.

"From the start this was a temporary arrangement, *n'est-ce pas*?" Athena spoke in a British accent festooned with French phrases and inflections.

"I feel used," he bellowed, looking at her severely.

"Did you not use me too?" Athena asked. "My home? My food? My bed? Now please use my front door and depart with dignity."

"I'll paint one masterpiece after the next," Dalton cried like a crazed revolutionary. "I'm Picasso! I'm Kandinsky! I'm Jackson fucking Pollock!"

"Don't forget to take your toiletries," Athena shrugged.

Freddy Hodge came to Athena's attention through Bitsy Woo, her personal assistant. While thumbing through a magazine in the reception area of her gynecologist's office, Bitsy came upon an article about Freddy and Wanda entitled *The Art of Mother and Son*. Accompanying the piece were photographs of Wanda's tattoo designs alongside Freddy's paintings. Bitsy was so struck by the boldness of Freddy's art, especially its riveting depiction of the relationship between food, sex and blood, that she took the magazine with her. Athena was impressed enough to request a meeting.

With its busted headlight and small hole in the floor on the passenger side, Wanda's old Plymouth puttered fifty miles to the affluent community of Beaux Facade Beach with Freddy in the driver's seat. As gray clouds swirled above, a genial security guard opened the front gate of Athena's sprawling estate. Freddy parked in the circular driveway that surrounded a dazzling, two-tier statuary fountain. The cascading water created a sound of pure tranquility. Freddy closed his eyes and listened, trying to calm his thumping heart.

His fist pounded on the solid oak door. As someone who never paid attention to fashion, Freddy felt grossly underdressed in his ragged jeans and T-shirt. Just walking on the premises seemed like a formal event. A wavy-haired French housekeeper opened the door, smiled coyly, and ushered him into the grand foyer.

The towering Athena breezed into the room, followed by three full-grown Great Danes. With one bejeweled hand extended and the other waving a Hermes scarf, she introduced herself and her dogs. Freddy was impressed and overwhelmed, awed by the surroundings. Then she took him on a grand tour of the eleven bedrooms and nine baths on two separate floors. Paintings of all sizes and styles dotted the walls. Sculptures weren't as numerous but were equally impressive. Finally, Athena summoned her guest to the Victorian sofa in the living room and held his gaze as they descended simultaneously.

"I take it you like my work," he said.

"It speaks to me," she responded. "You are renegade and original."

Despite their three inch height difference (she was taller) and twenty year age gap (she was older), there was a comfortable ease between them, a subtle recognition, as if they were members of some unique tribe.

"I've always been a renegade," he boasted.

"That's what makes you original."

The housekeeper entered the room with a pot of steaming coffee and a plate of chocolate croissants. She exited with a petulant swing of her hips.

It took five minutes and two croissants for Freddy to accept Athena's invitation to move into her home from August through January. "What's the catch?" he asked with suspicion. In his experience, everything came with at least one string attached.

"The catch is you have to paint for five hours every day," Athena explained. "And I own half the work you complete."

"I won't have to wash floors or haul heavy furniture?"

"*Mais non! Jamais!*" she snapped. "No, never."

There was an implicit understanding, made clear by Athena's gentle stroking of Freddy's hair, that he would share her king-size canopy bed. The novelty and perverse nature of the arrangement intrigued him.

"You're an enigma," Athena breathed to Freddy. "A pauper with the allure of a prince."

"Thanks," he replied. "Can I ask why you do this?"

Athena's face lit up with a knowing smile. She'd heard the question before. "*Bien sur,*" she chimed. "Why I do this. I do this *parce que*...because I adore creative people. I worship talent. And I am a connoisseur of great art. I search for the new Chagall, the next Matisse, the Toulouse-Lautrec of tomorrow."

"Cool," he said. "I've heard of them."

Freddy moved in the following afternoon.

Shaved fennel salad with Macadamia nut-crusted sea bass replaced corndogs and fries as Freddy's typical dinner. He had never even seen this kind of food. Meals were prepared by Athena's Cordon Bleu-trained chef Lucien, and served by a butler named German (though he was Russian) on large plates decorated with hand-painted Chinese figures. On their second evening together, Athena insisted on changing Freddy's name to Frederick Rhys-Hart.

"Definitely has class," he admitted. Later that night, he practiced his new signature for twenty minutes.

On their third night together, Athena lay topless on the bed while massaging Freddy's right foot. "Tell me why you paint, my darling," she said. "Please tell me from the deepest part of you."

Freddy explained that the moment his brush touched a canvas he felt a sublime rush. "To me, painting is fuckin' nourishment, sensuality. It's like this is what I was born for. When I'm not painting, I'm in a trance, obsessing about it."

Athena chuckled, moving her hands up to his ankle. "You sound like Monsieur Bacon. Francis was obsessed, too. I kept telling him to light up. He was so austere."

"I think you mean *lighten* up," he corrected her.

"Ah, yes."

Under the stimulation of his breathtaking new residence – the crashing waves on the beach, the cloud shadows that moved across the garden – Freddy created one magnificent piece of work after the next. His personal favorite was inspired by a particular rock from Athena's impressive rock garden. Gold and football-shaped, it actually shimmered in sunlight. Freddy was so dazzled by the rock that he found a special place for it in his studio.

During his stay at the estate, Freddy created two influential pieces acclaimed by art aficionados in three continents. About *Naked Laundress Flying Over Liverpool*, critic Jackson Wise wrote:

"Rhys-Hart's golden orange sky, perhaps the world on fire, reflects a frightening, post-apocalyptic universe. His loosely thrusting strokes are the carriers of idealism, symbols of the mad, limitless possibilities of the creative mind at work."

About *Prairie of the Wounded Prostitutes*, critic Lance Rubin wrote: "Rhys-Hart's new work is strangely reminiscent of Dali with the added influence of Degas, specifically the latter's deep psychological intimacy, found in his early family portraits. But Rhys-Hart's rebellious spirit looms large. Every detail shrieks of non-conformity thanks to either its bold color or magnified size."

Athena read this review to Freddy as they sipped pomegranate martinis.

"I could be the next Dali," he boasted.

"You already are, my sweet. Trust me, Salvador is rolling in his grave."

"Did you know him?" Freddy asked.

"Of course," Athena replied. "I was *tres jeune*, very young, he was *tres vieux*, very old, but we had a history together, quite a colorful one."

"What kind of history?" Freddy was fascinated.

"I became his muse. You know the word muse, *non*?"

"Yes I do. Of course. You're *my* muse."

Athena was visibly moved. "Hearing you say that warms my heart." She grabbed his forearm. *"Mon coeur s'ouvre a ta voix comme s'ouvrent les fleurs aux baiser de l'aurore.* My heart opens to your voice like the flowers open to the kisses of dawn."

"Cool," he responded.

One night after dinner, Freddy felt inspired to decorate the skin of his muse. He created a red, blue and black peacock on Athena's left calf. "Do you like it?" he asked with excitement.

"It speaks to me," she chirped. "Now, how do you say this..I want you to fuck me like it isn't tomorrow."

"You want me to fuck you like there's no tomorrow," he corrected her.

"*Voila!*"

"I can do that."

One hundred miles west, Dalton Rhys-Malone couldn't shake the humiliation of his banishment from Athena's estate, especially since he stopped taking his anti-psychotic medication. Adding insult to brutal injury, he found Freddy's work obvious and unoriginal.

In Dalton's first gallery showing since exiting Athena's house, critic Sander Videlle wrote: "Still using the brewery as his backdrop, the artist is stuck in a world that has lost its luster. The young women in *Ladies Bathing in Lager* look bored by their activity just as the scantily-clad servant girl does in *Rubbing Brown Ale on the Albino.* Even in the striking *Let's Scare Bonnie to the Brink of Death,* Mr. Rhys-Malone's spatial relations are off. The startled Bonnie, with her frightened eyes, appears infinitely larger than the two men attempting to stuff her into the mash tun. A promising talent neglected to keep his promise."

This scathing review pushed Dalton over the edge. The very day the critic's words appeared in print, the artist filled up the gas tank of his red Corvette and headed east, armed with a bag of beef jerky, a six-pack of Guinness, and a desire to set things straight.

When he arrived at the gate of Athena's manse, he faked a cheerful smile for the security guard he had gifted with bottles of brandy during his six-month stay. "Scutter, my man," Dalton crowed. "Would you believe I left one of my sketch pads on the side porch?"

"Not a problem," Scutter replied, reaching for the phone.

"Don't bother Miss Easterling. It's in the magazine rack. I don't even have to go into the house."

"All right then."

The electronic gate opened, and Dalton proceeded. He pulled up to the patio, then quickly slipped into the house through a side door. Freddy was exactly where Dalton expected him to be, in the studio, standing before his canvas, brush in hand.

With a demonic shine in his eyes, the wronged artist pulled out a nylon rope from his pocket and removed his shoes. He tiptoed into the room, approaching his rival from behind. Freddy continued working, oblivious that he was in the presence of a madman with the intent to kill. Dalton inched his way over, closer and closer, until he was only a few feet from his prey. In a sudden rush, he lunged at Freddy with maniacal force and wrapped the rope tightly around his neck. The shock on Freddy's face quickly turned to rage, and he used every bit of available strength to kick his attacker in the groin. Dalton wailed in pain like a wounded horse crashing to the floor.

As Freddy grabbed his golden football-shaped rock, the thrill of the fight came rushing back to him. He'd forgotten the primal joys of physical assault, the supreme satisfaction of proving one's strength. Freddy bashed the boulder into Dalton's head. The wild beast had been let out of its cage, and the sensation Freddy felt was as natural as sex. As he prepared to strike the finishing blow, Dalton shrieked, "Don't!"

"Why not?" Freddy asked. "You tried to choke me to death!" .

"Well, I was thinking about it."

"Is there any reason I shouldn't knock the shit out of you?" Without waiting for a response, the untamed human animal delivered the lethal blow just seconds before Athena rushed into the studio. "*Mon Dieu!*" she cried.

"Who the hell is this guy?" Freddy shouted. "He tried to kill me."

"An artist who lived here once," she replied with sadness. "He lived here just before you. And now he passed out here."

"Passed *on*," Freddy corrected her. "Is that Malone?"

"Yes. Dalton Rhys-Malone."

Freddy pleaded self-defense. The incident made headlines and became fodder for tabloid magazines and cable news networks.

The ensuing trial was nothing less than a media circus with crowds of frenzied onlookers gathered outside the courthouse each morning, holding signs that read either *Free Freddy!* or *Fry Freddy!* There was no denying that Frederick Rhys-Hart bludgeoned Dalton Rhys-Malone; the only question was motive.

It took the jury a mere twenty minutes to reach a verdict. The foreman, a lanky tree surgeon with grass stains on his rumpled shirt, solemnly announced: "We find the defendant, Frederick Rhys-Hart, not guilty."

Public outcry was immediate. Freddy's supporters cheered; his detractors chanted the name Dalton Rhys-Malone as they marched in candlelight vigils. Some in the media suspected the verdict was a result of Freddy's undeniable sex appeal. One of the jurors admitted to the Associated Press that she found Freddy "ferociously seductive."

Frederick Rhys-Hart changed his name back to Freddy Hodge and decided not to move back into the mansion, despite the five weeks remaining in his commitment. He explained that it was time to move on, free of entanglements and potential gossip. This stunning, mystifying news hit Athena like a meteor. She had fallen in love with her Wunderkind, something that had never happened with any of her previous proteges.

One month after this unsparing decision, Athena swallowed thirty sleeping pills with a strong pomegranate martini. She grabbed a kitchen knife and stepped into a tub filled with warm water and freesia scented bubbles. As she luxuriated in the bath, she lifted her leg and deliberately slashed her ankle, making a sizeable cut into her one and only tattoo. She rested her leg on the side of the tub so that she could watch her colorful peacock bleed to death. The water engulfed her.

Every new piece of work Freddy Hodge completed, whether a simple sketch in black and white or an elaborate painting in vibrant color, featured a willowy creature with a martini in one hand and a Hermes scarf in the other. Sometimes this intriguing figure was front and center; sometimes it was in the background camouflaged by color and light. But wherever it happened to be on the canvas, the eye of the beholder was undeniably, inexplicably drawn to it.

Kate's List of Lovers

Tracy and I were stretched out on the grass on one of those lazy days before class, and she asked me how many guys I've slept with. This was between bites of her Weight Watchers-approved apple. "I don't know," I told her, picking a blade of grass out of my hair.

"Don't you keep a list?"

"Well yeah," I replied, "but I never counted the names."

I knew that a lot of girls on campus kept a list, and most of them rated the guys on performance on a scale from one to ten. I didn't do that. "How many have you slept with?" I asked, playfully running that blade of grass down her ski-sloped nose.

"Three," she reported. "Rob, Michael, and Andy. Rob and Andy were tens, Michael a seven."

"Why did Michael fall short?"

"It was over too fast," she giggled. "I want to see your list."

"Why?"

"Because I'm too curious. I have to see it. Pleasepleaseplease."

I didn't feel like getting up, but it was obvious I couldn't calm Tracy down. I didn't really care if she saw the list, though it dawned on me that a few of the names could potentially shock her. But she was a big girl, and it was time for her to grow up, anyway.

We trudged up the stairs to my dorm room. In my underwear drawer, I took out a journal. From the journal, I removed a folded sheet of notebook paper and handed it obligingly to Tracy. She unfolded the paper, and quietly read aloud:

> Tommy Pratt
> Steve Wynter
> Dirk Lane
> Travers Most
> Christophe de Botton
> Robert Itkin
> Denis Smeal
> Tommy Louloudes
> Gabe Zelzah
> Renzo Barbetti
> Mercer Biddle
> Mauricio Pucci
> Nathaniel Lucci
> Micah Koenig
> C.J. Dorfman
> Kenny Calhoun
> Nicholas Craig
> Alexander Graham Hunt
> Aldo Valeri
> Theodore Sestanovich
> Rick Waller
> George Stormer
> Edwin Kadue
> Blake Dossick
> Raymond Oderman
> Alex Henahan
> Kyo Sato
> Father Joseph Parsons
> Matt Flack
> Matt Hornby
> Cesare Montagnani
> Joel Stein

Cal Scrogum
Hamish Eisenberg
Bobby Peet
Terry Pappas
Lawton von Behren
Damon Sayles
Harry Wissmann
Thaddeus Brayton
Senator Randall Rush
Bennett Brodsky
Rabbi David Geldzaller
Deon Higgins
A.J. Jiranek
Lou Quick
Link Hennessy
Jason Cook
Javier Longo
Gunga "Buzz" Narayana
Ben Fritzley D.D.S.
Jonny Lee Landers
Casper Tomkins
Benny Rust
Owen Lawrence
Lawrence Owen
Lew Laufer
 George "of the Jungle" McKenna
Lars Skoonabeek
Dave Reese
Brogan Hamm
Clark Davis
Arch Brown
Rocco Tuttle
Steve Brustein
Mauricio Ponti
Mike Alltop
Chad Oestrich
Jean-Paul Villand
Denny Schisgal
Nick Skouras
Martin Barton
Argyle Smollen

Tracy gingerly folded the paper and handed it back to me. "You had sex with all these guys?" she asked, aiming for nonchalance.

"Not at the same time," I told her.

"How does that make you feel?"

"It doesn't make me feel one way or another." It dawned on me that Tracy may have been envious. I never had trouble hooking up, but she may've encountered a bit of a hard time until she turned twenty and lost those pesky forty pounds. "Can we grab a bite?" I asked. "I could go for a salad and a glass of wine."

"I'm too unnerved to eat, Kate. Do you regret sleeping with any of them?" she inquired.

"I didn't get pregnant, none gave me a disease, and I'm ready for the next one. What's to regret?"

"Well, I look at sex differently than you," she said, squaring her shoulders and shifting her weight. "To me it's a bit more sacred."

"Sacred," I repeated. "I never felt sacred about giving a guy a blow job. You certainly can't accuse me of discrimination."

"No, your list would pass mustard at the United Nations."

"I think you mean pass muster."

"I like seeing the same guy over and over again."

"Then why aren't you with one of your chosen three?"

"Because they dumped me like last week's *TV Guide*." All of a sudden, tears began to stream down Tracy's cheeks. "I'm sorry," she whispered.

"Don't worry." I made my way back to her and wrapped my arms around her shoulders. "You'll find a guy who won't dump you."

"That's not it," she exploded, wrenching my arms from around her shoulders. "I'm crying because I don't think we can be friends anymore. I had no idea you were so loose."

"Loose?" I sputtered in disbelief. "What decade are you living in? The '50s? Call me easy or promiscuous or even wanton, but loose sounds like my skin is about to fall off."

"And wanton doesn't sound like a Chinese soup?" she snapped back with anger.

This sudden mood swing took me by surprise. I certainly didn't want to argue semantics. "OK, no wanton. Sorry. Call me loose, if you like. Pass the mustard, if you want."

"*Two* guys from Phillips Exeter Academy?" she asked in horror. "They were really cute."

Tracy took a few moments to collect herself. Then she crossed the room in four long strides, turned the door knob, and turned to face me. "For all intensive purposes, our friendship is over."

"Well, you can't have a one-sided friendship, so I guess it's over for me, too. For all intents, purposes, and whatever else there might've been."

"I won't mention the list to another living soul. But when we see each other in the hallways, let's pretend we don't know each other."

Tracy headed down the hall, her footsteps thundering after her. "I won't have to pretend," I whispered down the list. "Dave Reese." The name jumped out. "I think I'll give Dave a call."

We Knew What It Was By Then

GLASS DOORS SIGHED AND SHUT, floppy wet mops dampened dirty floors, stretchers wheeled past like room service tables en route to hungry hotel guests. Under bright fluorescent lights, a middle-aged nurse in crisp white approached. She gently took my hands and quietly, solemnly said, "I'm so sorry."

"Could you please increase his morphine?" I whispered to her. It was obvious his pain was becoming worse. The nurse nodded.

It was difficult to see him this way, but the difficulty wasn't mine. He didn't know where the gradual slide was taking him, where this vessel of sweat-soaked, urine-stained sheets would finally dock. Destination certainly not Barbados. Some of us knew where the journey would end; what we didn't know was exactly how he would cross over from this merry-go-round gone amuck. Questions couldn't be asked; the tour guide was on break. Drugs swimming through his barely thirty-year-old veins, it was only a matter of the enemy, a matter of time. Time made it worse, evil time. He suffered and gasped, cried out and hallucinated, struggled to stand up and escape, each day, each hour, more intensely, but with no self-pity. He was bravery personified. Only flashes of fear and occasional delirium illuminated the still-boyish face.

The rich, limpid sky outside the large window wasn't sky blue; it was azure. But it meant nothing. Friends stopped coming, they couldn't bear to see him this way, a virtual skeleton with protruding bones under a thin layer of flesh, his arms a kaleidoscope of blacks and blues and yellows from needles that plunged into his veins searching for blood. His body had become one giant side effect from the experimental drugs that were desperately trying but miserably failing, a barely-living organism with a T-cell count of exactly two when it should have been in the three digit range.

He was strangely beautiful, eyes as gloriously blue as the ocean, teeth white as snow-capped mountains. I couldn't leave because he was still fighting day fighting night fighting dusk fighting dawn fighting morning fighting afternoon and all the moments in between, fighting but never complaining, though the battle was ostensibly lost and the war was heading toward its inexorable conclusion. No peace treaty, no compromise. Sleep was a gift, but a fleeting, turbulent, constantly interrupted one. He was still holding on, though the train had arrived at the last station.

What do you do when you've given up, but the nightmare hasn't ended?

1988. We knew what it was by then.

We knew what to expect.

Fame & Madness in America

BRENDA

I don't deny killing him. Just look at the facts: He was alive one minute, dead the next. My husband of four days departed while dining with me in a dimly lit booth at Go Fish Grill, my favorite seafood restaurant. An autopsy revealed that Shawn Regal died of a lethal dose of horse tranquilizer. Microscopic remnants of the animal sedative were found on his dinner plate.

Shawn ordered the Chilean sea bass with red wine risotto and tiny white asparagus. I had the steamed cod in bok choy, and we were sipping an expensive, delicate Riesling. I made the decision to finish my steamed cod after Shawn was already dead, and this faux pas didn't go over well with the press, especially Mr. Jack Smith (who always struck me as having a sinister undertone). I'm sorry, but I don't believe in letting good food go to waste. Shawn had already devoured his sea bass, so I calmly finished my cod. I could have ordered dessert, but out of respect for the deceased, I passed. Did the press mention *that*? Of course not. And let me state in black and white: This restaurant has a tiramisu to die for.

Just before the heartless one's heart stopped beating, his head leaned back on the burgundy leather booth. On first glance, it appeared as if he'd fallen asleep. "Too much wine?" our attentive server Tessa quietly asked, observing the lifeless body beside me. I told her my hard-living husband had too much *everything*. When you have too much everything, you begin to think you're invincible.

I became a beaming bride and a grieving widow in less than a week.

BYRON, BROTHER-IN-LAW

The bitch murdered my brother. If she couldn't stand him, why didn't she just divorce him? Damn it, I told him to avoid Jewish girls.

Look, I come from a Jewish family so it's not like I'm prejudiced. I just prefer Gentile women. Like Brenda's friend Veronica Poplin. Veronica and I hit it off at Shawn and Brenda's wedding, but the affair was doomed once the bride poisoned the groom. I mean, how could you date a girl whose best friend murdered your brother, no matter how.

VERONICA, BEST FRIEND

I've known Brenda Bernstein since we were sophomores at Vassar. That's right, the murderess is a Vassar grad.

We spoke on the phone a dozen times a day, shopped for everything together, and watched chick flicks until four in the morning. I knew Brenda's taste in clothes, books, movies, music, linens and shampoo. I knew the kind of guys that made her weak – white collar – and she knew the kind of guys that made me drool – blue collar with tats.

Brenda Bernstein had the warmest heart of anyone I knew. If we saw a homeless person on the street, she wouldn't walk past without putting a five dollar bill in his tin can. She knew I loathed any form of exercise yet she managed to convince me to do a 10 K run with her for some charity. "I'll make the donation," I told her, "just don't make me do any actual running." But she explained that sweating along with the thousand other participants was an integral part of the experience. And she was right.

When I heard what Brenda did to Shawn, my jaw literally dropped. For the first time in our friendship, I thought she was lying. It turned out she wasn't.

ESTELLE, MOTHER

What did I do wrong? It has to be a mother's fault when *both* daughters turn out bad.

I don't mean to say marrying a black man is worse than killing a white one. The murder is much more severe. Still, when my daughter Fern says to me, "Ronald Epps and I are engaged," I had to consider it as some kind of rebellion. But against what? She had a lovely childhood.

So they became man and wife, gave me a light-skinned black granddaughter named Dina, and divorced before their ninth anniversary. I certainly didn't celebrate when the interracial marriage ended because you never want to see your child go through hell. But I was glad when Fern married Frank, a Caucasian fellow, even though Frank wasn't as intelligent or considerate as Ronald Epps. And Ronald Epps drove a nicer car. I could barely squeeze into Frank's two-door Toyota, but Ronald's Lexus had so much leg room and such comfortable seats. Leather.

Then there's my youngest. I was thrilled when Brenda finally says to me, "Let's go shopping for a wedding dress, Mom." Shawn Regal seemed like a sweet guy. Who could have predicted that four days after the wedding my daughter would poison him to death and wind up at the Forest Hills Correctional Facility for Women?

BRENDA

Every morning outside the courthouse, a large gaggle of women, all ages, races and sexual orientations, gathered 'round and chanted "Free Brenda!" They bravely held signs and banners that read *Prison's No Place for a Princess* and *Acquit or Eat Shit!* I waved to them and flashed the warmest smile I could muster.

It was gratifying to have good people on my side. It made me feel less alone in the cesspool I'd gotten myself into. But I *was* alone, and nobody was coming to my rescue.

I didn't mean to kill him. All I wanted to do was cause a little stomach discomfort for a couple of hours. But when you're dealing with horse tranquilizer, you have to be very, very careful.

JACK SMITH, REPORTER

Brenda was *my* story, just like Watergate was Woodward and Bernstein's. I covered it for the paper from day one. Not since the Octomom gave birth, Susan Boyle sang, Joran van der Sloot murdered, or Sully landed the plane in the Hudson had a story captured the public's imagination in such a frantic way. Women looked up to Brenda like she was some cherished icon, and guys wanted to see her get the chair.

Obviously, I was with the guys.

BRENDA

On a frigid December evening long before our nuptials, Shawn made a startling confession to me: He was not physically able to have sex more than one time in any twenty-four hour period. I certainly wasn't an expert on the subject of male erectile dysfunction, but I was pretty sure this wasn't normal. He'd always been this way, he explained, even as a randy teenager. I told him he should consult a doctor, but he was either too embarrassed or too ashamed, and in his thirty-three-year-old head, Viagra was not an option.

I'll now jump ahead to our wedding reception. (In time, this leap will make sense.) I asked my dashing groom if he knew the glamorous, size zero, six-foot-tall-in-heels blonde, because I certainly didn't. "That's Ingrid Vilhelmsdotter," he said, "the Finnish girl I went out with."

I was so stunned, so positively mortified to see this towering goddess at my wedding that for a few seconds I literally couldn't speak. Then my words emerged, loud and clear: "I thought you were finished with the Finnish girl."

"I am," he explained. "But that doesn't mean we can't still be friends, right?" I honestly didn't know if that was a rhetorical question, so I kept my mouth shut. "She wants to meet you," Shawn said. He took my hand and led me to Ingrid as the band played a tepid rendition of *Sunrise, Sunset*. Ingrid's striking, high-cheekboned face lit up when she saw us approaching. The three of us took part in polite, superficial banter that didn't make me feel any better about her presence.

Later, Veronica valiantly tried to cheer me up. "Look," she told me, "Shawn didn't choose to marry Miss Finland. He married *you*."

"Are you just saying that because you don't want this to ruin my wedding night?"

"Yes," she told me. That's what I loved about Veronica – she spoke the truth no matter how hurtful and tormenting.

What young, breathing couple doesn't make love on their wedding night?

We tried very hard, but hard was unfortunately lacking. Shawn just couldn't perform, blaming his lack of get-up-and-go on the excitement and nervousness of the wedding. I had my doubts. My head went straight to the fact that this was a guy who couldn't get it up more than once in any twenty-four-hour period. Since he hadn't had sex with me, I couldn't help wondering if he had it with someone else. To me, this was logical thinking.

"Who was it?" I asked in a deliberately playful tone. To my great surprise, Shawn took the question seriously, vehemently denying the accusation. But his dead serious response was a dead giveaway, and I could no longer hide my humiliation. "Who was it?" I repeated, this time distressingly. "Ingrid?"

"No!" he pleaded. "There was no sex."

"You were gone for half an hour at one point. Where did you go?"

"I don't remember," he said.

"Everyone was looking for you." I reminded him that lawyers are professional liars, and he needed to tell me the truth the whole truth and nothing but the goddam truth if he had any hope this marriage would last beyond the night. I threw a Tic-Tac into my dehydrated mouth, then tried a different tactic. "Whatever it is, sweetheart," I tenderly said, "I love you to death, and we'll work through it together."

My husband of less than eight hours turned his head away for what seemed like eight minutes. I had the feeling he would chalk up his failure to perform on some kind of post-party depression, and he would convey this to my face in a heartfelt manner. But when he finally spoke, when he confessed his crime, his eyes remained on the foot of the bed as if he were reading off a TelePrompTer. "Ingrid and I went for a short drive in her new car," he said. "The Volvo V50."

A short drive. He and Ingrid. In her V50, a model known for its comfort and versatility. "We did it one final time," he said, "for old time's sake, you know?"

I explained, rather calmly (I thought) in light of the situation, that "for old time's sake" traditionally meant enjoying a toast or singing a nostalgic song, not having sex with a leggy Nordic beauty in the back seat of her Swedish SUV. "There are certain rules of engagement you just don't break," I said.

"You're right. I'm very, very sorry." Shawn promised me, swore on his actual knees, that sex with Ingrid Vilhelmsdotter would never happen again. Without missing a beat, I promised *him* that our marriage would be annulled as quickly as possible.

"You're joking, right?" he asked.

"I wouldn't joke on my wedding night, Shawn."

"What'll we tell our guests?" he asked.

"Here's an idea," I said. "How about the truth? We'll explain that during the wedding reception, the groom rubbed a woman's vulva in her Volvo and that woman, as it turned out, wasn't the bride."

"Do we return the gifts?" he asked, more concerned about the wedding presents than he was about ending his marriage to the woman he supposedly loved.

"Well Shawn," I said, "frankly I don't think I can part with those stainless steel asparagus tongs."

That night, our memorable, extraordinary wedding night, my new husband slept on the sofa in our hotel suite as I sprawled out on the rose-colored sheets of the luxurious king-size bed, under the cotton duvet cover with its romantic floral pattern. Sleep was impossible, so I ate a juicy peach and a bunch of grapes, gazed out the window, and attempted to enjoy the fragrant flower arrangements that decorated the room.

The following morning, I watched my newlywed husband pack his belongings and move out of our apartment. His destination was of no interest to me. I didn't care if he was planning to move into temporary quarters at the Carlyle Hotel or sleep on a wooden bench on Central Park West. I didn't ask, and he didn't tell.

FERN, SISTER

The events of the week following Brenda's wedding were absolutely surreal for everyone involved, and they happened so fast it was virtually impossible to keep up. One minute Shawn moved out of the apartment, the next Brenda told me Shawn was dead, the next Brenda's face was plastered on the front pages of practically every newspaper in the tri-state area. The runaway train had left the station.

The phone didn't stop ringing. If it wasn't some reporter on the other end of the line, it was some distant relative or old acquaintance I hadn't spoken to in years. I couldn't go anywhere without being accosted by neighbors bursting with questions. People actually began to look at me differently, as if I might be a danger to the community like my sister was.

We were all aware of the presence of the media outside the courthouse, but none of us had any idea how far-reaching this trial would become. Every time someone appeared on the witness stand, his or her face graced (or disgraced) the cover of the following day's newspapers. Then the public determined who deserved their attention. Those they liked would appear in print and on nightly news programs again and again while those they detested would vanish from sight. The process was truly astonishing. Were people this starved for entertainment? Brenda's trial became their daily ritual, and the players in the trial became overnight celebrities. I had the distinct feeling these dances with fame would only grow more intense with time.

What struck me most profoundly was the fervent passion Brenda's story aroused.

People discussed the trial in bookstores, bakeries, coffee houses, restaurants. On buses, trains, TV talk shows. Mornings, nights, weekends. Sides were taken and minds were made up. We had become part of the zeitgeist.

The tabloids filled their pages with Brenda and company. Page Six routinely reported sightings of anyone connected with the trial (especially the beautiful Veronica and the beautiful Byron). Late-night TV hosts joked about the court proceedings. It was like every citizen had a unique relationship to my sister and the trial. She was an object of curiosity, a seemingly normal, respectable woman who carried out a peculiar and horrifying act.

I always believed things like this didn't happen to people like us. They happened to *other* people, other families, families that owned handguns. Now that it happened, our lives were changed forever.

PATSY KILPATRICK, NUT CASE

"I have a confession to make. I'm the one who killed Shawn Regal. It was me, Patsy Kilpatrick, who poisoned the handsome bastard."

This was the announcement I voluntarily made to the national press.

"I had a love/hate relationship with Shawn Regal, just like Brenda Bernstein did. He broke my heart the way he broke Brenda's. He obviously chose Brenda to tie the knot, but I still adored the guy and hoped to be with him someday, somehow.

"Yes, Brenda was sitting with him at the restaurant the night he stopped breathing, but it was me who snuck into the kitchen and poisoned his plate of food with the lethal tranquilizer. I decided to confess because the truth is very healing. If anyone is wondering, I'm wearing Stella McCartney, and the pumps are Kate Spade. No questions, please, and I ask you to respect my privacy at this terribly trying time."

BRENDA

"Patsy who?" I asked incredulously.

When my attorney Grace Lefkowitz-Caprice told me some twisted woman confessed to poisoning Shawn, my first reaction was disbelief. I was sitting next to Shawn through the entire meal. I saw the plate being lowered in front of him, I watched him chow down the Chilean sea bass, I witnessed his rapid decline. How was it possible that Patsy Kilpatrick poisoned him? The broad was nowhere in sight!

My second reaction was raucous laughter. I guffawed a full thirty seconds. "She must be so dizzy she can't stand up unless she holds onto something," I hooted.

My third reaction was gratitude. "Why not?" I asked. "Throw her in the slammer and set me free!" If this was what the woman wanted, who was I to deny it to her? Unfortunately, Grace told me it wasn't so simple, that there needed to be proof of Patsy's involvement. And we knew Patsy's involvement was all in Patsy's demented mind.

A quick investigation of Patsy Kilpatrick showed that she was an actress, real name Ruth Ann Rott, originally from Peru, Indiana, with a resume that included a flop of an off-Broadway musical, a regional TV commercial for an acne ointment, a national commercial for deodorant, and several auto shows in Detroit. (Her task was to point to cars while wearing a bathing suit and heels.)

Before arriving in New York, she stopped off in Hubbard, Ohio for a few months to stay with her ailing Aunt Eileen. While there, Ruth Ann was arrested for disorderly conduct at a square dance and spent a day in jail. When Aunt Eileen departed, Ruth Ann took the elderly woman's cash, pills and first edition copy of *Lady Chatterley's Lover,* and hit the road. She landed a job as a waitress in a bowling alley in Bowling Green, then decided to go for broke and head to New York. In the end, I realized the publicity-hungry Patsy was using me merely for self-promotion.

But so was everybody else.

GRACE LEFKOWITZ-CAPRICE, ATTORNEY

I explained to my very perplexed client that in high-profile cases, you can expect at least one or two certified lunatics to come forward and confess to the crime, people who have a frantic, pathological need for fame. It happens every time, and the press swarms around these narcissistic sociopaths. Their every move is covered by the tabloids and the cable news networks before it's revealed that their story is bogus. Then they vanish from sight, and a week later nobody can remember their name.

VERONICA, BEST FRIEND

Visiting Brenda in prison was a very trying experience. Couldn't somebody take a bottle of Windex and wipe the damn glass partition?

The fact that I never wanted to stay more than five or ten minutes made me feel terribly guilty. I loved seeing Brenda, but I detested the prison milieu. I grabbed any excuse to leave: a business appointment, a lunch date, abdominal pains.

Just *getting* there took the better part of an hour. On account of the visits and the trial, my schedule was becoming impossible. I had to ask my editor for an extension on my piece *Refrigerated Cabinets for Your Cashmere,* which I thankfully got.

BYRON, BROTHER-IN-LAW

At least *one* good thing happened since my brother was poisoned by that bitch. I got a call from someone at *People* magazine, and they wanted to include me as one of their Fifty Most Beautiful. (They loved me on *The Rachel Maddow Show.*) Photo shoots, interviews, morning TV appearances, the works. It was weird how everybody involved in Shawn's killing was making a killing for themselves, enjoying their fifteen minutes of killer fame. I was determined to stretch mine to at least a couple of hours.

VERONICA, BEST FRIEND

Byron wasn't the only one being pursued by the media. Journalists hounded me night and day, wanting to know every detail of my friendship with the accused. I did lengthy interviews with *USA Today, the Los Angeles Times, the Philadelphia Enquirer, Newsweek, Redbook, Town & Country, the Sacramento Bee, Nurse Practitioner, MSNBC, the Chicago Sun-Times,* and *Modern Bride.* An editor at *Playboy* offered me a sizeable hunk of cash to do a nude photo spread. The amount was more than I made in a year, but in the end I decided to pass; I didn't want my future children to see me virtually naked.

BRENDA

My mother visited me in jail every other day, usually bearing gifts: a few chocolate chips cookies, a loaf of rye bread, a large babka & rugelach crate from Zabar's. The chocolate babka and cinnamon rugelach were out of this world delicious, but I begged her to stop with the edible presents.

When Veronica visited, she brought no gifts, only news. "You won't believe this," she gushed. "I was watching TV last night, and all of a sudden I heard your name."

I braced myself. "In what context?"

"Well," she said with a proud grin, "next week is *Brenda Bernstein Week* on Lifetime. Every night at nine o'clock they'll be showing a movie where a woman murders her husband. Did you know about this?"

"No," I said. "I hadn't heard this thrilling piece of news."

"Do they have to pay you for something like that?"

"No," I explained. "I've become a public figure, so my pathetic life is fair game."

Veronica leaned back on her chair and took a deep, satisfied breath. "It's astonishing, isn't it? One day you're completely unknown, and the next you have a whole week devoted to you on Lifetime."

"Only in America," I said. "The land of opportunity."

"Absolutely. Is there someplace to get a large chai latte around here?"

BYRON, BROTHER-IN-LAW

The offer came from out of the blue: a hosting gig on a new dating series in development. The producer saw me on MSNBC and thought I had what it took. The show involved pairing up the brothers and sisters of people who were savagely murdered. The idea was that these guys and gals have gone through so much pain that they deserve to be matched up with *other* people who've lost a sibling in a violent death.

The fact that my brother was poisoned by a horse tranquilizer obviously qualified me to host the series, but I asked the producer Winnie Zing why she chose me out of all the other surviving siblings. "Because you're hot," she said. "If *you* can't make a girl forget about her murdered sibling, no one can." I wondered if I'd have to fuck her at some point as a way of showing my gratitude.

To be honest, hosting a game show wasn't my top choice for my first job in the biz. I would've preferred a good part in a movie or even a second banana role in a sit-com. But the money was great, and I thought the exposure would've been awesome.

The show was originally called *No Slain, No Gain*. Then it was changed to *He's Dead, She's Dead*. Then the powers that be finally decided on *Mating After Murder*. That has a great ring to it.

FERN, SISTER

Fame used to be reserved for the extraordinarily talented or the highly respected. Often, these people used their notoriety for worthy causes, humanitarian efforts. But now, I witnessed talent-challenged men and women using their notoriety from my sister's trial for one cause only: to become more famous. It used to be that *sex* was the national obsession. But fame undoubtedly replaced it. Fame is the new sex.

BRENDA

"I have something exciting for you," my mother said as she pulled out the latest issue of *Time* magazine from her hefty handbag. "Have you seen it?"

"No," I said. To my astonishment, it was my face, the face I've known intimately for thirty-one years, that was gracing the cover. This weekly space, ordinarily saved for heads of state, rock stars, movie stars, breakthroughs in medical science, and stories like *How We Became Human, What Doctors Hate About Hospitals, Dropout Nation,* and *The Radical Mind of Thomas Jefferson,* featured me, Brenda Bernstein! I knew that some journalist from the magazine interviewed my mother, Veronica and Grace, but it didn't dawn on me that the piece might become a cover story. (I declined to be interviewed as I've declined every single offer.) Underneath my face were the words: *Women Who Kill.*

Lovely, I thought. Would any female be happy about going down in history as one of the *Women Who Kill?* I really wish they'd come up with a better title. Some people might've thought I went on a carefree shooting spree, gunning down anyone in my path. Others might've lumped me in a category with "Squeaky" Fromm and Aileen Wuornos. I was not a woman with a .38 Special. I poisoned one solitary time under one specific circumstance. Thankfully, the article itself explained the real story, and in the end I came across in a fairly sympathetic light – as a strong, confident woman who decided to put my foot down when my husband's behavior became intolerable.

According to the piece (and to several women-on-the-street who were interviewed), it doesn't get much worse than a groom having sex with a woman other than his new wife while his wedding reception is taking place.

The piece obviously painted a ghastly picture of Shawn. In fact, no one in the Regal family was presented in a flattering light. Byron was called "a spoiled rich pretty-boy with no obvious talent except attracting some of New York's hottest women" and Isabel was described as "one of those wealthy East Side doyennes who wants to be taken seriously as a patron of the arts but all she's really serious about is what to wear for lunch at Café Des Artistes." (The accompanying photo of Isabel was actually taken at Jean Georges.) Even the Regal patriarch, Murray, was mentioned; his decade-old scandal which ended with a self-inflicted gunshot wound seemed especially tragic now that his oldest son was dead too.

There was a bit of fascinating insight from Veronica. She said, "You don't really know what you're capable of until you're right there, in the moment, facing something you never thought you'd face. I never would have dreamed Brenda Bernstein could do something like this."

I never dreamed I'd be on the cover of *Time*; who does except maybe a president or a rock star or a president's mistress? I couldn't help wondering if I would be chosen *Time*'s Person of the Year.

ESTELLE, MOTHER

I bought all the issues of Time from the corner newsstand, around thirty of them. I proudly told the guy behind the counter, "That's my daughter on the cover." He looked at me strangely, then he says to me, "She's a woman who kills?" I told him to shut up and read the article. Then I dragged myself to another newsstand two blocks north and bought all those issues too, around forty. You'd think they'd give you a discount when you buy in bulk, but they don't. "Times are tough," the scruffy guy behind the counter says to me.

They chose a beautiful shot of Brenda for the cover and there are some lovely pictures of her inside: her sweet sixteen, college graduation, Brenda in court, Brenda being led to prison. She looked stunning in every shot, and it was fun to compare the different hair styles she had through the years.

How many people can say they have a daughter who was on the cover of Time? No matter what, my little girl made the world stand up and pay attention. Not everyone might agree with what she did, but she sure got noticed. I brought two dozen issues to the courthouse and had Brenda sign them. What a fantastic gift one of these would make! For so many different occasions.

FERN, SISTER

Time and time again I declined to be interviewed by *Time*. (They asked me three times.) I had no interest in seeing my name or face on any printed page. My mother, on the other hand, as well as a half dozen of Brenda's acquaintances, would've *paid* the publication to be included.

What does this say about us as a species? Would most of us grab hold of fame like starving vultures? Is the possibility of stardom so powerful that it overshadows everything we value in our lives? Maybe we read too many tabloids, watch too much television, and care so much about the rich and momentarily famous that we long to be one of them. My reticence was the exception to the rule, and this was ironic because during my drug days I would've loved the attention. But at this point in my life, quite frankly, I was astonished and ashamed at the behavior of just about everyone I knew.

When I asked Veronica why she decided to go for the publicity instead of maintaining a low profile, she explained that we were all given this one chance, probably the only chance we'd have in our lifetime, to garner the world's attention. As one of the chosen few, she felt she should take advantage of this gift, maybe even use it to further good causes. I told her I thought that sounded well and good but I didn't see many charitable acts being performed as a result of anyone's newfound fame. "Give it time," she told me. "I, for one, would definitely appear on a telethon. But altruism aside, don't you love going to clubs like Bungalow 8 or the Beatrice Inn or Soho House and getting VIP treatment?"

"Of course," I said with sarcasm. "I adore the VIP treatment I've been getting at the trendy night spots."

Out of curiosity, I Googled my sister's name. I was astounded by what I found on page after page after page: fan sites, photo galleries, bios, daily blogs, mug shots, memorabilia, quotes, transcripts, lists, analyses, late-night jokes. There were YouTube videos and TMZ reports. Someone researched our family tree and discovered we were distantly related to Pearl S. Buck, Johann Sebastian Bach, and Glenn Beck. (That's a Buck, a Bach, and a Beck.) A guy was peddling a book called *What To Expect When You Poison A Spouse*. It was hard to believe the Bernstein clan (and Brenda in particular) had become so utterly fascinating to the world at large.

By the end of week number three of my sister's trial, I prayed this wouldn't go on much longer. But I had a strong suspicion that some other more publicity-hungry people hoped it would forge on forever.

LISA GHERARDINI, EX-CLASSMATE

Brenda Bernstein and I sat next to one another in our sixth grade class until I asked Mrs. Voskevic if I could move to the back of the room.

Our bitter rift began when Brenda refused to believe I was named after the Mona Lisa. The enigmatic woman in Leonardo DaVinci's famous painting is supposed to have been Lisa Gherardini, the wife of a Florentine silk merchant. My parents were aware of this art history trivia because Gherardini is our family name. When I was born, they decided to give me the first name of Lisa.

For some reason unbeknownst to me, Brenda thought I was making the Mona Lisa story up to draw attention to myself. What she failed to realize was that I didn't need to invent stories to draw attention. Being the prettiest girl in class (in the whole school, actually), I received more attention than I could handle. It was obvious Brenda was consumed with jealousy. She was also jealous that my father was a millionaire real estate mogul and that my hair wasn't frizzy and I had a summer house.

I remember it was cold, snowy day when the incident happened. I was eating lunch in the school cafeteria along with everybody else. I took a sip of my grape juice and it tasted funny so I immediately took a bite of my egg salad sandwich to drown out the taste. But I was really thirsty so I took a few more sips of the juice. Then I felt sick. Horribly sick. So sick that I had to be rushed to the hospital.

When I wasn't looking, someone had poured ink into my glass of grape juice.

If I had taken just a few more sips, I would've died. My two precious children would not have been born. To this day, my tongue is slightly blue in color. Brenda never admitted doing the deed, but I always felt she was the culprit. The girl had a penchant for poison. When I heard that she was on trial for killing her newlywed husband with a horse tranquilizer, I felt I had to come forward and enlighten the jury. I knew this woman was guilty as sin. In fact, Brenda Bernstein was sin personified.

BRENDA

The prosecution was thrilled that Lisa Gherardini was delivered to their doorstep, a living, breathing example of my poisonous instincts. With her testimony, some people felt that the final nail had been hammered into the Brenda Bernstein coffin.

It's mind-boggling that someone who was a total bitch at age nine could be an even bigger one at thirty-two. You'd think life would've softened her, age might've had a mellowing effect. Instead, Lisa Gherardini hardened: her features, her personality, maybe her arteries for all I knew and hoped. Behind that phony smile, beneath that oversize green jade bead "Flintstones" necklace and those cosmetically enhanced breasts, lived pure, unadulterated evil.

Every few minutes she glanced over at me with absolute loathing. I wondered what kind of person holds a grudge for more than twenty years.

Even though the jury seemed to look down at what I did to Lisa in elementary school, they appeared amused by it. Grace Lefkowitz-Caprice, on the other hand, seemed like she was ready to strangle me.

When Lisa was finished, she stepped down and walked out of the courtroom with a petulant swing of her hips. For a fleeting moment her eyes met mine, and she could tell I was hoping her husband would poison her.

Her testimony caused irreparable damage to the defense, Grace explained. I asked her if she could attack Lisa's character and credibility the way she did with that lunatic Patsy Kilpatrick. "We've researched her," Grace told me. "The woman's record is as immaculate as her Armani suit."

"Are adults responsible for what they might've done when they were eight?" I asked.

"Not necessarily. But their actions just add another shade to their character."

During Lisa's testimony, I experienced what some might call an out-of-body experience. I was able to step back and get an objective view of what was taking place. There was a certain splendor and grandiosity to the courtroom proceedings. All these people, the jurors, the lawyers, the bailiff, the courtroom deputy, the court reporter, the judge, were gathered together on account of *me*! I felt intimidated by the spectacle, the pomp and ceremony. I felt small and unworthy, like a novice violinist suddenly playing with the London Philharmonic. I wanted to stand up and shout, "I'm not worth this trouble!" But I knew there were certain people present who felt that I *was*. These enemies had a single, powerful purpose: to put me away for life.

BYRON, BROTHER-IN-LAW

I could hardly believe the truly thrilling news. I predicted a movie would be made about my brother's life and death but I never would've predicted *three* of them! Three fucking films! Two for television (ABC and TNT) and one for the big screen, directed by the great Oliver Stone.

I obviously wanted to be in the Stone version. I definitely wanted to at least meet the guy and read for him. I didn't think any actor could be more right to play me than me. I looked like me, talked like me, thought like me. But I realized Stone could have a whole different concept of Byron Regal for the role. If he thought I was more suited to play Shawn, I would've gone along with that.

GRACE LEFKOWITZ-CAPRICE, ATTORNEY

In all my years as an attorney, I had never been so unsure of a jury's decision. Usually my instinct is right on the money, but this time I wasn't placing any bets.

The only thing going for us was the public. Masses of women who'd been emotionally hurt or blatantly humiliated by husbands and boyfriends were seriously rooting for Brenda; her case had become a cause célèbre. Brenda Bernstein was a new feminist hero, a strong, passionate woman of conviction who put her foot down when her newlywed husband performed an unforgivable act. No matter how many times the jury was told to ignore the public outcry, it was virtually impossible to do so. Brenda's face was everywhere. She had become synonymous with equality for women.

BRENDA

It is exasperating, nerve-racking, tormenting to wait for a jury's verdict. Your very life is in their hands. Your entire future, everything you've strived for, is at stake. Twelve hideously dressed people you never met will decide your fate – a dozen people with tics, faults, perversities, hidden prejudices, perhaps eating disorders, drinking problems, and very weird tastes in music.

Grace told me the wait could be a matter of hours or days or weeks. I asked her if I could possibly bring a large plate of desserts into the jury room. Or maybe I could help some of the female jurors with their make-up. She shot the second idea down even faster than the first.

BYRON, BROTHER-IN-LAW

That fucking moronic jury. What the hell was taking them so long? Brenda killed my brother; what was there to figure out? She was as guilty as any inmate on death row.

At least the game show took my mind off the trial a little bit. Two producers were on board: Winnie Stall and Jordan Bromstad. Sometimes during our off time, Jordan and I hung out. (Winnie was married with kids so she zoomed home at the end of every day.) Jordan was gay and single. He could talk about movies or music or politics or books or music. The only thing he didn't know about was sports. I knew about sports, so we balanced each other out.

Jordan wasn't bad looking, but obviously when we went out someplace all eyes were on *me*. It didn't bother him because I was the star of his show. What I liked about him was that he didn't come on to me. Some gay guys try to seduce me even though they know I'm straight as an arrow, but it never happened with Jordan, not even once, not even when it was really late and we had a lot to drink and I hugged him goodnight. You gotta have respect for a guy who represses his burning hot sexual desires.

BRENDA

That damn jury had been deliberating for thirteen endless days. My idea about supplying refreshments was replaced with the desire to enter the jury room and strangle each and every one of them.

I assumed they were doing this to me deliberately, purposely, willfully, with unmitigated malice - stretching this deliberation to give me as much anguish as humanly possible. These people were sadists. Probably for the first time in their lives, they had complete power and wanted to relish every second of it. So far, thirteen days and counting. Almost two entire weeks.

Then, finally, the verdict was in. We were all called back to the courtroom.

"This has been an extraordinarily difficult and complicated case," Judge Kiki Kestenbaum declared. "Unprecedented. Throughout the trial, the media coverage has been overwhelming. The defendant's action touched a nerve. Everyone involved in this case became a media celebrity, and some have parlayed their newfound fame into on-camera careers. This is a case that will certainly be noted in the history books as it has been widely discussed in the tabloids.

"Will the foreman please step up?" Judge Kestenbaum finally requested. The foreman of the jury turned out to be Juror #4, the one I thought could be either a man or a woman. "Has the jury unanimously agreed on a verdict?"

"Yes, we have."

"Do you find Miss Brenda Bernstein guilty or not guilty?"

"We, the jury," he said, and it was definitely a male voice we were listening to, "find the defendant, Brenda Bernstein…" And for some ungodly reason, the goon paused. For what? Dramatic effect? Was he auditioning for a production of *Twelve Angry Men?* Why would someone pause at that precise moment? Punching him in the face was all I could think about, no matter what the verdict was.

"…we find Brenda Bernstein…not guilty."

A deafening cheer swept over the courtroom like a giant, cleansing wave. I felt hands and arms and fingers on me, voices coming at me from all directions. Tears of joy streamed down my face. The ideal was over. Fini. Das ende.

I was now yesterday's news. We *all* were. And I couldn't have been happier.

GARRETT SOCOL, a native New Yorker, currently resides in Los Angeles. His first life was lived as Gary Socol, and he was a television producer. Gary created and produced "Talk Soup" (host, Greg Kinnear) and "The Gossip Show" among other series for E! The specials he wrote and produced were hosted by Joan Collins, Jenny McCarthy, Jerry Springer, Molly Ringwald & Ally Sheedy, Carnie Wilson, Pamela Anderson, Jaime Pressly, Tori Spelling and others. His first play The Shadow of Greatness premiered at the Berkshire Theatre Festival in 2000 in a production that starred Richard Chamberlain. His second play Bicoastal Woman enjoyed a successful run at the Pasadena Playhouse.

His second life began in 2007 when he left television and began writing fiction. His short stories have been published in dozens of literary journals including *PANK, Perigee, Pear Noir, The Barcelona Review, The Dublin Quarterly, Underground Voices, > kill author, 3:AM Magazine, Hobart, Drunken Boat,* and *McSweeney's Internet Tendency.*

www.ingramcontent.com/pod-product-compliance
Lightning Source LLC
Chambersburg PA
CBHW050316110726
47899CB00007B/2259